WILLNOT

WILLNOT

A Novel

JAMES SALLIS

BLOOMSBURY

NEW YORK · LONDON · OXFORD · NEW DELHI · SYDNEY

Bloomsbury USA
An imprint of Bloomsbury Publishing Plc

1385 Broadway	50 Bedford Square
New York	London
NY 10018	WC1B 3DP
USA	UK

www.bloomsbury.com

BLOOMSBURY and the Diana logo are trademarks of Bloomsbury
Publishing Plc

First published 2016

ISBN: HB: 978-1-63286-452-9
          ePub: 978-1-63286-454-3

LIBRARY OF CONGRESS CATALOGING-IN-PUBLICATION DATA
Sallis, James, 1944–
Willnot : a novel / James Sallis.—First edition.
pages ; cm
ISBN 978-1-63286-452-9 (hardcover : acid-free paper)—
ISBN 978-1-63286-454-3 (ebook)   1. Physicians (General practice)—Fiction.
2. City and town life—Virginia—Fiction.   3. Murder—Investigation—Fiction.
I. Title.
PS3569.A462W55 2016
813'.54—dc23
2015025305

2 4 6 8 10 9 7 5 3 1

Typeset by RefineCatch Limited, Bungay, Suffolk
Printed and bound in the U.S.A. by Berryville Graphics, Inc., Berryville, Virginia

To find out more about our authors and books visit www.bloomsbury.com.
Here you will find extracts, author interviews, details of forthcoming events,
and the option to sign up for our newsletters.

To the gang

Bob, Camo, Little Girl,
Fox, Squirrel, Ritz,
Sophie, Missy

Grace, of course

And in memory of Blackness,
Charley, Marmalade

And especially Dragon

Hang me, oh hang me,
I'll be dead and gone . . .
Don't mind the hanging,
it's the waiting around so long.

Traditional song

1

WE FOUND THE bodies two miles outside town, near the old gravel pit. Tom Bales was out on an early-morning hunt when his dog Mattie dropped the quail she was retrieving, sprinted to a stretch of worried earth, and wouldn't budge. He'd call, she'd start toward him and circle right back, barking. It was the smell that got him finally, when he walked over. Mushroomy, dark. Cellarlike.

The clearing was eleven by thirteen, roughly the size of a room in the 1950s-built houses we have in abundance, bordered by black walnuts and oaks. The surface was sunk in a bit, scored with unnatural right-angle cuts as though large shovels had been working it. Runners of kudzu and gnarled vines teased the edges.

Sheriff's men had been the first to respond once Tom went back to his truck and called it in on his cell phone. One of them pulled an old army-surplus folding shovel out of his truck and started digging. The smell got stronger and stronger. He'd been at it twenty minutes or so when he hit bones.

By the time Andrew and I pulled in, Sheriff Hobbes himself was there with prisoners, two black, one Hispanic, a heavily tattooed white, along to do the digging. We stood watching as dirt piled up behind them. State had brought their dogs, but this being Mattie's territory, things hadn't gone well with that, so those two were back in the van glaring out the windows and slobbering at them.

"Someone's been out here hauling off dirt again," Sheriff Hobbes said, "and lots of it. Thought we had put a stop to that."

"It's not like we don't have plenty of dirt."

"Dirt costs money. Out here, nobody's sure who owns the land. Some get to thinking that means it's free for the taking. Bo Campbell again, most likely. Him and his so-called construction company."

"We used to swim out here when I was a kid," Andrew said.

Errant dirt scattered across my shoes, his boots. I looked over at the gravel pit: scooped-out cliff, bulldozer gulleys, dry flats, rock.

"And pretend we were exploring Mars, yeah, back in the day." I'd had a crush on Trudy Mayfield. Told her I was going to be an astronaut.

"Sorry to pull you out of OR." Andrew wasn't great at meeting eyes, but this time he did. "Thought you should see."

"I've been after Ellie's gallbladder for close on two years. No reason you have to go on being sick, I kept telling her. It'll wait a while longer."

"She's gonna be red-hot mad."

"That she is."

"She's right good at being mad."

"Some have the gift."

I really didn't know whether Andrew was a pet project of mine or I of his. I'd been caring for him since he was twelve. Diagnosed ADD when his parents brought him in for troubles at school, started him on the drugs that were high on the pop charts at the time, then had second thoughts and set him up with an old classmate getting great results with behavioral therapy. Mostly it worked. These days, Andrew pretty much single-handedly ran the local ambulance service as well as Elmer Kline's mortuary. Kline was close to eighty, terminally addled, periodically found walking down Main Street in the early morning with only mismatched socks on. Andrew wasn't licensed as a mortician, but we didn't pay a lot of attention to such things in Willnot.

At some point Andrew had decided that, since I understood so well what he was going through, I had to be ADD too, that they just hadn't known what it was back in my day, so there was a connection between us. Never could figure out if he wanted me to own up to it, or simply had in mind giving me traveler's tips. My reflexive first thought, of course, was *classic projection*. But when I open those blinds and peer behind, all I can think is how shallow our explanations and understandings are.

"That lime I'm smelling now?" Sheriff Hobbes said.

Andrew scuffed at the ground with a bootheel. "How many you think there are?"

"Bodies?"

He nodded.

"First ones weren't far down. Could be just those."

"Or a hole full of them," he said. "And there's the lime."

"Right. Wouldn't want to waste expensive quicklime on just a few bodies."

Andrew thought I was joking but he wasn't sure. He sort of half laughed then shook his head, covering both bases. "Sheriff Roy says eighty years ago this used to be rich meadowland."

"Eighty years from now it may be again. And no one will remember any of this."

We heard it before we felt it. Tiny shushing sounds as rain-drops hit leaves high in the trees. Then puffs of soil as they struck bare ground.

Andrew looked up. "Oh, great! Just what we need." Mattie was running in circles, snapping at raindrops and growling.

Minutes later it had all gone to mud.

As I squished and dripped and puddled my way through the front office, Maryanne eyed me over the top of her glasses. *Gleeking*, Andrew calls it. Maryanne's half my age but often watches me the way my mother used to, a mix of bemusement and tolerance, what's the boy up to this time?

I keep a change of clothes in the back. You never know when you'll get called out to view a pit full of bodies and get rained on. Running shoes, chinos a size or two too large, and a pink chambray shirt with frayed collar doesn't make much of a fashion statement, but Maryanne had already given me the look.

She smiled, tolerance having moved to the front of the line, when I came out.

"Ellie was giving them hell. The anesthesiologist says he almost went ahead and put her to sleep to shut her up."

"Stand-ins have a hard time of it. It's me she wants to give hell."

"They told her what happened, where you were. She quieted down some." Maryanne nodded to the side room, part closet, part kitchen and break room. "Coffee's fresh enough to pass. I moved all your appointments, didn't know how long you might be out there."

"Gordie Blythe up for anesthesia?"

"Who else?"

"Think he's still around?"

"I can check. You want me to see if the rest of the OR team's available while I'm at it?"

"Please."

I grabbed a coffee while she made the call, stood looking out a window the size of a chessboard at a wren industriously plucking tendrils of vine from the chain-link fence out back. Minutes later, Maryanne was at the doorway.

"Not gonna work. Ellie's gone home. 'Just took up and left,' the charge nurse says. Want me to call her?"

"I'll do it tomorrow. And since the cupboard's bare, why don't you go on home too. Take the rest of the day off."

"I was working on billings."

"They'll wait."

"You sure?"

"About that, yes. Run. Claim your freedom. I'll shut everything down."

Minutes later, desk drawer sliding on rails, open, shut, she was out of there, thanking me even as she flipped open her phone to call Sarah and say they could have a late lunch if she hadn't yet eaten and was of a mind to.

I refilled my cup, then, settling at the desk, spilled coffee on the mess of papers bird-nested there. Articles from medical journals that I hadn't got around to reading and never would, transcribed examination reports from before I began doing most everything on computer, blurry faxes of lab work I'd long ago acted on, panhandling letters from professional organizations, charity duns, catalogs.

It's possible that something registered subliminally, a sound, a subtle shift in light or shadow, but if so I can't recall it. I looked up, and a man stood in the office doorway. He had entered by what I believed to be a locked door, crossed the front office, broached my own door—and how long had he been standing there?—without my once being aware of him.

He wore jeans with a whitish line down the front bespeaking years of pressed creases, a dark shirt, brown corduroy sport coat. Casual black lace-ups, scuffed, good leather.

"May I come in?"

"Academic at this point, isn't it."

Closer, he glanced at the chair across from my desk and back at me. When I nodded, he sat.

Cars passed on the street outside. Out in the front office a window rattled. Generations of insects died.

"You don't remember me. Brandon." Momentarily he shut his eyes, relaxed his face, let his head fall back. "I used to sleep a lot."

Brandon Roemer Lowndes. Sixteen when he wound up at the wrong end of a prank gone horribly south. Left town on the school's band bus for a football game twenty miles away, came back six days later in an ambulance and a coma. I'd taken care of him for close to a year, touch and go at first, then the long plateau and rehab. One of those strange mirrors life can throw up to you.

"You're looking good, Brandon," I said.

"These days I go by Bobby. And you're looking a little old around the edges, Doc. Used."

"From in here too."

"It's this place, this town. Sucks the life out of you. I got away."

"You did."

"Marines. Just in time for two undeclared wars."

"And now you're back."

"Briefly," he said. "Passing through."

Passing through were the first words he spoke when coming out of the coma. He'd said that twice, *Passing through*, *Passing through*, then opened his eyes and looked around, asked where he was. No way he was going to forget that. So he'd chosen the phrase for effect. Like saying *I used to sleep a lot.*

"Business? Visiting old friends?" Both parents were dead, the single sibling, a sister, living in Canada, last I heard.

"Don't have much by way of business these days. Never had old friends. Nothing here but rust and memories."

"Yet here you are."

He stood. "Just wanted to come by, tell you hello."

I got up and said it was good to see him, went to the office door with him and, when I heard the front door close, walked back to the window. He stopped half a block down by Ellie's resale shop, Rags N Riches. Old Ezra was out there. No one knew much about Ezra. A mountain man, some said, others holding out for plumb crazy, twice a veteran, or all of the above. He showed up from time to time, lived on the streets, never asked for money or food but gratefully accepted what was given. By silent agreement the whole town watched after him.

Bobby stood talking to Ezra, then pulled out his wallet and handed Ezra a sheaf of bills. Ezra tucked the money away in the pocket of the innermost of three shirts he was wearing and shook Bobby's hand. They walked their separate ways.

Bobby had a limp. All but imperceptible, but there. No drag, so probably not neurological. Didn't have the stutter and hitch of a bad hip or knee. And deep, permanent, not a simple sprain or torn tendon. An old break maybe, with loss of bone so that one leg was slightly longer.

I watched till he turned the corner onto Mulberry. Then I double-checked to be sure the door was locked and went to make fresh coffee.

2

THAT WAS TUESDAY. Wednesday we're sitting at the table over breakfast and Richard asks, "What happened yesterday? Everybody's talking about it."

"Everybody's talking about it and you don't know what happened?"

"I don't mean what they found. What happened?"

I shook my head.

An old song played on the radio, *storms never last do they baby,* and when Richard said "Well yeah, they do," it took me a moment to realize he was speaking to the radio.

"They were killed?" he said, turning back to me.

"Buried, at any rate. And together. We may never know why."

"Or who." He fished the tea bag out of his cup with index and second finger, let it swing and drip. "That will be a sacred place now. Not in the religious sense." He set the tea bag on his plate. "The kind of place people go, thinking that being there will help them understand things."

Richard doesn't see things the way others do. He's a teacher. "Yeah, that's us," he said not long after we met, "a cliché from old Westerns. Doc and the schoolmarm. Well, except for the marm part." I often wonder what students make of his sidelong looks and reality reboots. In radiology, we're told there are no right angles in nature; we see them on X-rays, something's wrong. In Richard's world, right and oblique angles are everywhere.

His latest rescue lay at his feet. Actually *on* his feet, since the cat often confused shoes with pillows. Because Dickens looked at you only when you spoke, Richard thought he was blind. And he runs into walls, Richard said. Only once or twice, I maintained. Maybe he's just slow to learn, or not too bright.

The first save was a bird. Richard came in from school with it, one of his kids had found it on the schoolyard. "So?" I said as he held it out to me. Richard: "You're a doctor, right? A healer?" I bound the wing and while the bird never flew again, Miss Wrengali had a pretty good life for a year or so in the backyard.

Richard got up and took his dishes to the sink, Dickens indignant at being dislodged. "What's your day look like?"

"The usual. Save a few lives. Curse the darkness. Eat lunch."

"Might you find time in there to run Dickens by Doctor Levy, have him checked out?"

"And what, put it on your tab?"

"I could pay you back."

"In kind, I presume."

"Or you have my credit-card number."

"I do. So does Doctor Levy. As does Lands' End, Best Buy, Fry's, the Humane Society, Cordon Blue's, NPR . . ."

"Funny man."

"Just an observer. But sure, I'll take the old boy in."

"You think he's old?"

I looked down at Dickens, sound asleep again, feet straight

out in front of him, chin flat on them. "With all his frantic running about? No way."

"You do know they have claws, right? And can suck the breath out of you as you sleep? I have to get dressed and off to school. Told the receptionist at Doc Levy's you'd be in around nine."

"Of course you did."

He blew me a kiss from the doorway.

"Decided to take the day off, did we? Do whatever it is you young folks do these days?"

I bit into the cookie she'd served with my coffee. It shattered with a thunderous snap, parts thudding onto my lap, others skittering roachlike across the floor. Good bet she'd had the package in her cupboard, to be brought out for visitors, for years. She took no notice.

Intended, I think, as a smile, her upper lip lifted from the center. "Don't mind me, Lamar. I know where you were."

"Yes, ma'am."

"More coffee?"—which may not have been of the same vintage as the cookie, but wasn't far off.

"Thank you, no, Miss Ellie. I was wondering when we could reschedule your surgery."

"Lord, don't you think we have enough bodies for the time being?" She laughed, not at her joke, but at my expression. "You shouldn't take things so seriously."

"My parents always said the same thing."

"Along with teachers, a horde of other adults, and friends who were close enough to say such, would be my guess."

I nodded.

"And here you are, all grown up. Removing bad parts from

people, stitching and stapling them back together, propping them up. Serious stuff."

"I understand that you were angry, Miss Ellie, and I do apologize."

"I wasn't angry, Lamar." She grew quiet then, and I sat wondering how I'd never before sensed, past all the salty-dog rhetoric and rodomontade, the calm surrounding her. "I was . . . reminded." Definitely a smile this time. "A good thing to be reminded. We should hire people to do that for us. A new career choice."

She stood. Rather spryly, all things considered.

"The South did well by you, young man, but manners have their limits. There's no need to go on pretending you'll drink that abominable excuse for coffee."

I put the cup and saucer down, pushed them minutely away. She walked to a bookshelf threaded with figurines of shepherds, cherubs and carolers, held up a bottle of drugstore bourbon.

"I don't suppose you'll be joining me, this time of day?"

"No, ma'am."

She poured what looked to be precisely an inch and a half of whiskey into a glass that resembled, more than anything else, the holder for a votive candle, and rejoined me. "You lived here as a child, didn't you?"

"When I was fourteen. But only for a year, before my father moved us on. Moving on was what he did."

"I was eighteen when I came. Not a cent to my name, stars in my eyes. Two summer dresses and a brokeback pair of saddle oxfords. Five years before that, I'd come home from school, got the sandwich my mother left for me in the refrigerator for a snack, did math and history homework, listened to the radio. Around five, I went out and sat on the front porch to wait for my parents to come home. They never did.

"To this day I don't know what happened to them. I got sent to a juvenile facility, then to a foster home, Sven and Carey Waters. That's what they did for a living, but they were good, kind people. They raised me, other kids coming in and out, in and out, all the time. When I was eighteen, I left."

"I didn't know that."

"No reason you would."

"Did you stay in touch with them?"

"Just a postcard or two, those first years. But when I started getting onto what they'd done for me, seeing that, understanding it, I began writing letters. Every week, just about. The two of them had done everything together, and they died the same way, within days of one another, must be better than forty years ago now."

"I'm sorry, Miss Ellie."

"Nothing to be sorry about. Sven and Carey took good care of me, taught me independence, I've had a fine life. Unlike those people out there by the gravel pit. It got me to thinking, is all. People disappearing. Families. How some of us find our way and most never do.

"A friend I had back then, when I heard the Waterses had died, she told me 'They've passed on to their reward, Ellie.' I looked at her a long time and said, 'You ever think about what you're saying, or you just open your mouth and let words fall out?' Nell never cared much for me after that. But you can't fix stupid. And you sure as hell can't kill it."

She finished off her whiskey, picked up my cup and saucer. "Thinking I'll wait a spell on that operation, Lamar. Doesn't seem the time for it just now."

I told her I understood, we'd talk later. Outside, the air was crisp and clear, still bearing witness to yesterday's rain, and the sun was bright. I thought back to my psych rotation as an intern. William Johnson, "Mister Bill" to everyone, fingers twisted like roots, half a leg gone to diabetes, half his mind gone to bad whiskey. "Look up there," he said to me one day on the yard, hand quivering—left, right, up, down—as he did his best to point, "that old sun's grinning like a fool."

Maryanne was not grinning.

"Stephen's back." She shook her head. No doubt whatsoever about what she was thinking. "I put him in your office, hope that's okay."

"Of course."

With Stephen you never knew what to expect. He could as easily be sitting quietly staring at the wall, down on hands and knees picking lint out of the carpet, or pacing about the room.

I tapped at the door, took a breath and went in.

Option number one, more or less.

"Close, Doctor Hale. I'm close."

Stephen was twenty-three. When he was eighteen, his parents and sister died in a car crash, hit and run. He was supposed to have been in the car as well but had begged off. Over the next couple of years we watched Stephen pass from wanting to find the person responsible, to believing that the crash was intentional, not an accident at all, but willful murder. *The boy's gone gumshoe,* as Richard said, Stephen's time so given over to his obsession that he'd abandoned friends, personal hygiene, regular meals and health, then lost his job. Almost lost the house as well, before an anonymous benefactor stepped in.

"That's good, Stephen. And what will you do now?"

"Whatever it takes."

14

"We've talked about this. Of all the ways it can end, none of them are good. Closure is for jars, books, and closet doors. What you have to do is start taking care of yourself."

"I will. After."

Trying for informality, even a bit of intimacy, I'd been standing by the desk; now I sat.

"So why are you here, Stephen?"

His eyes came silently to me and there we were, smack in the middle of our personal version of Nietzsche's eternal recurrence.

"I won't give you something to take the edge off. You know that. And you know how uncomfortable I am with being asked."

"It's what you do, Doc."

"No. It's not. I'm a mechanic, a tinkerer. I fix things, do my best to get them back in working order."

He smiled, the boy I'd once known surfacing briefly. "That's all I'm asking. I'm so close, Doc, I have to keep at it. But five, six times a day I look around and don't know where I am, how I got there. Or my legs start trembling, like I'm about to go down. Have to grab at walls, a table."

"Standard-issue anxiety, Stephen. Just like pain, loss, sadness, fear. Your body strikes back if you overuse it. So does your mind."

"Some nights I can feel myself going away, hissing or leaking out of my own body, like gas. Hear my teeth rattling like dice in a cup."

Anxiety. Dissociation. The words came easily. We attach them to processes, they migrate to the people themselves, and we think: Now I understand. But we don't, and the words themselves interdict further attempts to do so.

Maryanne broke the silence, hurrying through the door to say she was sorry to disturb us. Twelve-year-old Jenny Broyles crowded in behind her, brother Dave behind Jenny.

"There's a problem."

Jenny held her hands out as she came up to the desk. "It got hit."

"We don't know what kind it is," Dave said.

"A mockingbird," I said. Its beak had been torn away, one wing broken. Its eyes were dull. My mother had loved mockingbirds.

"We were at the park. It flew by, then fell."

"We didn't know what happened. Mr. Edmonds was there—practicing his swing, he said. One of his golf balls hit it."

I told them I wasn't much of a vet but would do what I could and took the bird into an exam room. When Maryanne joined me, I shook my head. Held the mockingbird in my palm and felt, or imagined I felt, the last beat of its tiny heart against my skin.

I went out and told the kids. By the time I got back to the office, Stephen had left.

Sam Phillips was waiting for his yearly insurance physical, so we took care of that: EKG, vitals and medication check, orders for lab work and CXR, followed by my usual recommendation that he schedule a stress test with the hospital and by my annual advice, rather more strident this time, that, given his age and family history, he really, *really* should have a colonoscopy.

A run of quick calls followed. Nancy Meyers, the school nurse, brought in a couple of third-graders to be checked for what she feared might be measles but was a simple rash, probably allergic. Dan Baumgarden came for a two-week checkup and dressing change; I told him he'd soon be able to say good-bye to the drains and catheter. Mary Withers asked if I'd mind whittling her corns down to manageable size again. John Crabbe needed refills on his Tenormin and Zocor. I kept telling him the pharmacy would call me for approval and renew, but he came anyway, every three months. I suspected I might be his only social contact.

That was, mostly, my afternoon. About four, I started looking through the piles on my desk and found a mass mailing from one of those pay-for-your-funeral insurance things. Mail the tear-off back in and you'd receive full information, a valuable booklet to help you plan, and a journal into which you could record *My Final Wishes*. The mailing came addressed to my mother, who would have had much to say about such folderol, codswallop, hogwash, and bull.

Sheriff Hobbes was sitting on the bench by my car having a smoke when I came out. Sheepishly he extinguished the cigarette on his boot sole and held it up. "More filter than tobacco."

"Still get the job done."

"Yeah, guess it will, at that." He fingered the butt to be sure no fire was left and tossed it in the trash container by the bench. The bench was spackled with pigeon shit. The container had Keep Willnot Clean stenciled on the side.

"Through for the day, Doc?"

"Never can say for sure, but I'm giving it a shot."

"Don't suppose you'd be up for a cup of coffee."

"Best get on home, Richard's expecting me. My turn to cook."

"Man administers to the sick and needy and cooks too."

"Let's not talk about success rates at either. Is there something I can do for you, Sheriff?"

Loose skin beneath his eyes, hunch to his shoulders. He'd slept poorly, or not at all. "You were out there, Lamar. What do you think?"

"I think we found a hole in the ground with bodies in it. There's not a lot more to be thought at this point, rationally."

"But you have to wonder."

17

"I wonder about most everything. How cruelty never declines, how it is that we're using everything up at such a headlong rate, why people have to have big daddies in the sky."

The sheriff sat, bull's-eye in the worst swirl of dried pigeon shit. What the hell. I joined him on the bench. "You know," he said, and after a moment went on, "I ever looked ahead, what I saw was maybe twenty years of writing tickets, cooling down domestic disputes, scaring kids who were on their way to trouble, investigating the occasional traffic accident—I'm good at that, know what to measure, what to make of the numbers. But this . . ."

"Not many of us wind up where we thought we would."

He shook his head. "Scares the piss out of me, Lamar. Not the bodies, not whatever happened out there. Not knowing what to do—*that* scares me. It's like you open up a book and discover you can't read, all the little hooks and curls don't make sense to you anymore."

Grady Faim's ancient Ford came chugging up the street, front bumper lashed on with wire and more or less swinging free. The pickup stopped, its window wound down, Grady grinned out at us.

"And here to our left, ladies and gentlemen, we have two pillars of the community—such as it is, such as they are—hard at work helping make our tiny corner of the world a better place."

"You want to move along there, Grady? Stop blocking traffic?"

"Don't see as there's traffic to block."

"You counted up your unpaid tickets lately?"

"No sir. But I have ever' one."

The two of them had never got along. Grady, a fantasist and aggressive paranoid, couldn't bear authority figures of any sort. And the sheriff had little tolerance for people who refused (as he said) to live in the real world. But the sheriff chose silence and Grady, faced with no further challenge, continued on. We watched his head bobbing about in the back window.

"There goes yet another full-tilt character in a mile-long daisy chain of them," the sheriff said. "They do abound. You ever figure out why so many kooks wind up living here?"

I stood and brushed at the seat of my pants. "We are, after all, a town rich with uncommon history."

That night in my dreams I'm working on a bridge. Girded with a harness that smells of sweat and machine oil, throwing myself over the edge of cement platforms and blindly into darkness, the harness plucking me from the fall with bone-jarring exactitude. Each time it does so, it seems that I partially surface from the dream, and the half-awake, half-aware part of my mind ponders how symbolic this all is.

At 3 AM both parts of the brain awoke fully when Dickens the cat climbed into bed with us and started puking.

3

"DOCTOR LEVY SAID he was okay."

"He is. Animals get sick sometimes, they throw up. Just like people. Not to mention their fondness for hair balls."

Morning again. Tiny sparks of flint in Richard's eyes, a hint of dark clouds at kitchen's edge.

"And he's fine now. Back to normal." Curled up at our feet, front paws twitching as he pursued gazelles, antelope and cans of premium cat food across ancient savannas.

"You don't know that."

Sometimes Richard brings out the preacher lurking deep inside me. "I don't *know* anything. It's all on faith, grasshopper."

And as I swallowed coffee, memory flipped back through its pages.

"I rarely see a tree without thinking about it falling," Richard said once as we were out driving. We'd met three weeks before that, when he came to look at an apartment one of my friends was letting. Doug went off to get keys and I asked the prospective renter what he was up to. Oh, you know, he said, figuring out who I am, what I want to do with my life, what kind of cereal to buy.

Then: Not really. Just looking for a place to stash my books and records.

"So," he said that day after the falling-tree remark, "if you're looking for someone to save—"

"Not that, or to be saved." The two so often go together. "Not on my list at all."

"What is on your list?"

"I'm not sure. But it's a short one."

Richard half wandered to the counter, got the pot, came back and poured what was left into our cups, taking care to distribute it equally. "So you think Dickens is okay?"

"I do."

He finished his coffee in a gulp. "Can I fix you breakfast?"

"The sheriff asked me to meet him at Sammy's."

"Oh, goody. A chance to get your grease quotient up."

"He wants to go out to the site."

"*The site.* You need to pause dramatically before those words, splice in organ music under." He went to the refrigerator, came back peering into a container of yogurt. "Two questions. He wants you with him why?"

"I haven't a clue. Next?"

Richard tilted the container toward me. "Did it look like this the last time we opened it?"

The site suggested a cross between a spectacularly disorganized Boy Scout campout, a sweat-your-way-to-glory religious revival, and a tent sale for big-box electronics. As though all three had mistakenly rented out the same space for the weekend and each refused to budge. A state trooper the sheriff knew came out to meet us.

The guy running the circus looked to be about fourteen. He caught my expression, said "I know, I get that a lot," and reeled off a résumé of past work: Bosnia, New Orleans, Sudan. When I asked him where he was based, he pointed to a battered green trunk, the kind we used to haul off to college with us.

"Sebastian Daiche," he said, the *ch* sounding as *sh*. "Everyone calls me Seb." Again he effortlessly read my face and responded to the unvoiced question. "Canada, originally. But originally was a long while back."

I wondered then how one gets into such work, and toward the end of the tour I found out. The summer after his sophomore year he'd worked on an archaeological dig. Three weeks along, they came upon what they thought might be the ruins of an ancient temple embedded in a hillside and, as they began to work their way farther in, the whole thing collapsed, hillside, temple and all, slamming down around them. Sebastian helped sort the remains of fellow workers. He seemed to have a knack for it, he said, "and we tend to stay with what we're good at."

Heads and bodies moved in, out and about, but Seb's core team seemed to be four.

Cliff Janeck, his direct assistant, thirtyish, one of those people so full of implicit energy that afterward you swear you saw sparks coming off. He'd say something, you'd look around to respond, and Cliff would be gone.

Heather Van Meter, self-described "computer overlord" and chief cataloger. "You want to get the Heather jokes out of the way now or later?" she said when we met. I told her my name in turn, she smiled and said "Sorry about that" with not a wisp of sympathy in her voice.

Marshall Wellman, a stray bit of archetype gone live, the little wiry guy who beats hell out of three big ones who take him for an easy mark. Virtually immobile, not even the eyes moving till he's up and about, then just as quickly it's over. He's the oldest of all the team, and everything about him bespeaks a hard-core military background. He's the noncom who actually runs the base, the assistant producer who does the heavy lifting. Even Seb deferred to him.

Leslie Shafer, resembling nothing so much as a Texas churchman even to the flop-over hair and pastel sport coat, but here holding down Materials Management. The entire department all on his own, Cliff Janeck said. Keeps count of the body bags and canisters, Heather said.

An arbor of scaffolding had bloomed above the hole. Beyond that lay a reef of canopies, recording equipment, storage racks and breakaway tables. Computers and clipboards everywhere.

"Redundancy," Seb explained. "We're accustomed to working in places where nothing can be depended on. Theft, pilferage, power outages, destructive weather, dissident troops, government or police confiscation. Every piece, fragment and sliver of information we gather is copied and recopied. On the hour, all the data's packaged back to the mains in Tucson."

We spent the morning out there, getting the tour, meeting members of the team, witness to the scratch and scrabble. Before we left we made a final visit to the hole. It had by now become a crater, strung with marker ribbons and depth flags.

"Four to six bodies, we're thinking," Seb said, "but no way we can know till we've tallied and matched parts. It was a stew down there."

Years in the far past, on Bastille Day, I stood in a Confederate cemetery with my father, magnolia detritus showering down on our shoulders, him saying "Be very quiet, very still, and you can almost feel the earth pulling at your body. Lines of force

24

forming around you." He had taken to reading poetry, a practice that thankfully proved short lived, though the fallout persisted.

Six hours in the future I sat at home listening to Richard say "The man's an idiot. An absolute, irredeemable, inexorable idiot. It's not just that he's incompetent, he doesn't give a shit. Not about the teachers, not about the kids."

"You can always quit."

"And what, spend my day tidying up the house, buying figurines on eBay?" He had the laptop on the coffee table and was working away at it even as he railed. Pages came and went. "I love my job, Lamar." Scrolling down. Then a flurry of keystrokes.

"No you don't. You love teaching. The rest of it, the endless meetings, the drudge of record keeping, mandated testing, breakroom politics, you despise."

"It all comes in the gift box."

"As, for the time being, does your principal."

"Listen to this." Without taking his eye off the screen he reached for his wineglass, realized it was empty, and held it up for a refill.

How can you know what you believe? From the day you're born, everyone is busy filling your eyes, ears and mind with what *they* believe, with information about how you're supposed to act, what you are, what you should be. The blanket's blue: you're a boy. Act like a man. Let us pray. It's all around you, streaming from parents, relatives, school, movies, music, church, TV, ads, the Internet. You breathe it in, it wicks up through your feet. Filling you up, pulling you in so many directions you can't walk straight, keeping you so distracted that you never have time to think.

"The kid's twelve, Lamar. Twelve years old and he thinks like that, writes like that. Father was killed in Iraq. His mother sees after Nathan and his sister on what she makes as a waitress."

"The diner out by the highway?"

"That's the one."

"I know his mother, then. I've heard her talk about her husband and kids."

"Last thing he wrote was on ant mills, about army ants that get separated from the main party, lose the pheromone track, and simply go on following one another, round and round in the same circle till they die of exhaustion. The circumference of one ant mill was measured at twelve hundred feet. It took each ant two and a half hours to make a single trip around."

"Cheery stuff."

"Actually he's a happy, easygoing kid. But he's thinking. Feeling. Reaching. And everything around him seems to be doing its best to squash that."

"And isn't that why *you're* there?"

Richard took a breath. "Of course it is. So easy to forget."

"Just as the boy said, distractions. And while you're sitting here remembering, I'm off to do a load of clothes. Brought most of a hillside back with me from the site. And my shoes are twice the size they were Tuesday when I put them on."

Dickens followed me to the utility room. He'd once caught a mouse out there, in the space between dryer and wall. I'd taken it away from him and put it outside, but Dickens figured time was ripe for another.

4

I WAS A great disappointment to my father. A writer, he never voiced it yet seems to have held hard to the clandestine notion that somehow I'd follow him into the breach. This dynasty of two sitting upright at our keyboards pecking away at the world's disorder one sentence at a time. There was silence on the evening I told my parents, over dinner, that I'd been accepted to premed. Finally, finished and about to rise, my father pushed his plate away and said simply, Good luck, Son.

He wrote paperback novels, science fiction mostly, though earlier he'd had his hand into mysteries, suspense novels, romances, historicals, even soft porn. As far as I know, he never counted, and copies had long since flown the shelves; from the Internet there look to have been ten, maybe twelve, of these. But with science fiction he found his niche. Three books in, he was being invited to conventions with names like FenCon or SlanDom. Two more and, at least at smaller venues, he became guest of honor.

These books *were* on the shelves. With one in particular, *Prophets of Duum*, I spent many a childhood hour staring at the buxom woman turned sideways as, from the border, emerged a monster with vast eyes, behind these two a herd of plants with tiny gnarled feet who or which appeared to be cheering—either the monster's attack or the woman's flight. By the time I was in med school, Joseph M. Hale books had overgrown the shelves and tumbled, nevermore to be seen, into boxes in various garages, mudrooms, basements, and sheds. From time to time he or Mom would think to send me one.

The earliest that I remember sold for 35¢, later ones for $4.95. The covers themselves never changed much. Blurb sources migrated from Anthony Boucher, to Ted Sturgeon, Judy Merrill and Fritz Leiber, folks I knew from conventions I was dragged along to at age four, ten or fifteen, to writers I'd never heard of, growing loftier and more breathless with each passing year.

Then the decline. Joseph M. Hale, "author of sixty-six novels and untold short stories, a classic in his field, a giant," staggering off, with a stray book published on the cheap here, another there, to the sunset of OP, out of print. Writers—artists—are commodities. And commodities get used up.

But that was years later. At the time I was in med school, then in internship and residency, my father was cranking them out to an audience ever hungry for more, publishing as many as eight or nine books a year under his own and other names, making, even at $750 or a couple grand per, good money.

And moving around. Always moving around.

Life must be lived forward but can only be understood backward—Kierkegaard, right? Right up there with "Those who don't know history" and "fifteen minutes of fame" on the top-cliché list of journalists and bloggers, though generally unattributed. The truth is that life can't be understood at all. Looking back now, though, it does seem that with every few books Joseph M. Hale became something of a different person. There was, in Boston, the uncomplicated craftsman, a carpenter who worked with paragraphs and pages rather than lumber, planes and nails. In Bend, Oregon, the heroic novelist swimming heartily upstream of literary fashion. J. M. Hale from Fort Worth, Texas, with a newfound bent for regional writing, laboring away at a rickety card table, expending as much time moving table and chair about in an effort to avoid direct sunlight as he did writing. And here outside Willnot, Joe M. the populist, a man of the people who within the year, taking it to the limit, had uprooted us yet again, to the undiscovered country of hills and hollers to live among squirrel eaters.

Someone said of Hemingway that each new novel required a new wife. Joseph M. Hale may have needed new screen doors. Longed for, hankered for, hungered for, had lust in his heart for new screen doors, and for new flies outside them.

Plenty of flies in those hills and hollers. Hunters nailed squirrels to trees, gutted them and stripped the flesh out, left innards and skins behind. The buzz and drone of flies filled my sleep for years after.

We lived in a house that a local modeled after a photo he'd seen in a magazine (*Life*, one imagines) and built "with his own two hands, tree to lumber to roof and floor and walls." It was a California bungalow gone wildly wrong: flush to the ground with earth showing between planks, proportions all out of whack, none of the corners met true, stand in the front room drooling and drool would soon enough fetch up against the kitchen baseboard.

Mother set about making, on a Singer that swiveled up magically from what moments before had been a table, our clothes. One morning weeks after we took up homesteading there, my father and I stood on the porch peering through windows the glass of which removed all angles from the world, bending them into gentle curves. Guided by the tissue-thin paper pattern pinned to it, Mother snipped away at a panel of pale blue cloth on its way to becoming my sister's new dress. I had voiced some typically snide adolescent remark about her enterprise.

"You think what I do is any different, Lamar? I string things together to make patterns. Things for people to wear. Maybe that helps keep them warm or feel better about themselves, maybe helps them believe there's some kind of meaning to it all. All I'm doing is picking stuff up and putting it somewhere else."

Mother looked up then, smiled and waved. Through the imperfect glass her hand seemed to have an extra finger.

"But Clara actually makes things, things that haven't been in the world before."

"Like clothes."

"Like this family."

Man of the people. Simple patternmaker. Literary outrider and trickster. A magpie sniping from other birds' nests. Yet he had quietly longed for me to follow in his footsteps.

Historians cobble up counterfeit accounts of the past, reducing thousands of streams to a dozen currents, overwriting actual lives, the stories of all those people simply wanting to get on in the world they know, with narratives of grand ideas and motives. Our stabs at understanding character are built of the same doubtful materials. We worry out a few select strands from an individual's life, a baker's dozen of dominant traits, and use these to form a portrait. When we are all seething masses of contradictions. And of surprise.

5

I WAS AWAKE with no idea why. 6:28 on the nightstand clock. First thought: Dickens throwing up again. Or Richard was having one of his sleepless nights. Then I heard the banging.

The front door opened. Voices.

Richard leaning into the room.

"It's the sheriff, Lamar." Then, with a mock-horror face, "My God, what have you done?"

I swung out and stood.

"Nice," Richard said, "but you might want to put a robe on. You know, go formal."

I grabbed his off the back of the door and went out.

"Sorry, Doc. You're needed. I could have called but figured it's faster this way. There's been an accident at the site."

Raising his voice, he continued as I went back into the bedroom to find clothes.

"Looks like a generator blew. Things were stacked up tight, so it took some containers and shelving with it. Only two workers on the scene that early. One of them's got what looks like a piece of rebar in his chest, the other's leg got hacked up pretty bad, lost a lot of blood. Wellman came in early and found them."

I shouted through the door. "They're at the hospital?"

"Andrew and his new driver transported, guy supposed to have been a paramedic up in Detroit? Kid said it was some of the best first aid he'd ever seen."

"Battlefield medicine."

"Probab*lee*."

Hours later, undressed and dressed yet again, feet hurting in my $400 cross-trainers that I still called tennis shoes, I asked for more suction. Janis Banks was running the table. Melinda Arnold was circulating.

Gordie Blythe looked up from his nice stool at the head of the table. "BP's holding fine, Lamar."

"Always good to hear. And while we're on the subject of hearing, who picked today's music?"

Dolly, our surgical orderly, raised her gloved hand. "Flutes from the Andes. Or maybe American Indian, I'm not sure. Beautiful, huh?"

Commentary circled the table—

"Very interesting," complete with trilled *r*'s.

"Unworldly."

"Ethereal."

—and came back to me. "Sounds like an asthmatic cat, one maybe the size of a cow, trying to breathe."

Dolly's eyes went wide. "You can't see it, but under this mask I'm making my little-girl face. A moue, or whatever it's called."

"It's okay, I like cats fine. And Richard's asthmatic." I bent closer. "What is that?" I pushed flesh aside with the edge of the scalpel. "Can you get a retractor in there?"

Gordie leaned in on his stool. "What?"

The man's leg had been struck by two, perhaps three pieces of jagged metal. One had slammed against the knee, ripped away skin but done, as far as I could see, no joint damage. From a gash farther down, tibia peeked out. Another metal piece hit high, close to the hip. That was my field. I was checking for bleeders. And I was seeing the border of something pale and amorphous.

"Do we have this man's history?"

"Only basics, from his personnel file."

As Janis scissored the retractor, I saw what I was half expecting. Gordie had come around from his stool and stood by me looking down. "That's a proud one," he said. A tumor on the order of four kilograms, snuggled up low in the abdominal cavity, tucked away there like an old sock at the back of a drawer.

I probed at the mass.

"I wouldn't be leaning in too hard on it, Lamar," Gordie said. "That femoral looks right thin."

And about to erode. Gordie had called it. Ten days from now, or a month, or two, it would have given way and the man would have bled out in minutes.

"How providential that we all happen to be standing here," I said, "with time on our hands. Shall we have this little bugger out?"

Within the hour Mr. Patmore lay in recovery, trussed, ticked like a mattress with stitches, pillow-propped, pale and befuddled. I explained it all to him once he was awake, then again a couple of hours later in his room. The tumor, I was able to tell him subsequently, was benign.

Wellman and Seb Daiche sat in the waiting room outside Recovery, Wellman watching TV with no affect, as though it were broadcasting in some language he didn't know, Seb punching away at the keys of a laptop. I ran it down again for them after telling Wellman he'd done good work out there. He looked at me much the same as he had at the TV and nodded.

"Good," Seb said. "Not to worry. The foundation will cover all expenses."

"You have a foundation?"

"Work for one. That's the only way we're able to do what we do. Nonprofit, straightforward agenda, no doctrinal or direct government ties."

I didn't miss Wellman's reaction to that: an all but imperceptible turn of his head.

Sammy Cohen, who had been taking care of the other casualty in the adjoining OR, was in the surgery lounge self-medicating with a tumbler of orange juice. We compared notes. Improbably, a hollow aluminum shaft from shelving had skirted heart, lungs and major vessels, the boy'd be good to go in a week. I told Sammy what Seb had said about the foundation.

"Damn. If only I'd known . . ."

"What, you'd have used the expensive thread?"

"Instead of fishing line, yeah."

Not a lot was left of the day, or of me either (how did I ever make it through internship and residency?), but after checking post-op X-rays and lab work, I swung by the office. Had a couple of feverish kids, a possible bowel obstruction, a case of carpal tunnel waiting for me. And an FBI agent named Ogden.

"We don't often see federal agents," I said as she followed me into my office. "Or ever."

"Considering what you have outside town, you may have to get used to it."

"That's why you're here?"

She didn't respond.

I sat, smiled, and waited. She remained standing.

"I believe you know Brandon Lowndes?"

"Of course I do. I took care of him when he was a child, and very ill. He goes by Bobby now, I understand. What do you go by?"

"Why would you want to know that?"

"Not many have two names hereabouts. Just our way. First or last, that's it. The occasional epithet. Crazy Jane, Dago Frank. All meant respectfully, of course."

She swept my face for a clue that wasn't there.

"Theodora, but most everyone calls me Teddy."

"*Most everyone*. And a bit of hill-country lag buried deep. West Virginia?"

"North Carolina. That was a long time ago."

"So was my association with Brandon."

"Have you recently seen or been contacted by Sergeant Lowndes, Doctor?"

"A direct question. Things are looking up here. Why don't you have a seat, Theodora Ogden? Surely federal agents aren't prohibited from sitting during an interrogation."

"This is not an interrogation."

But she sat, not demurely, sinking easily into the chair and pulling her feet close. None of the usual fidgets with clothing, posture, where to put hands.

"He was here three days ago," I said.

"For what reason?"

"Just to say hello, he told me."

"That doesn't make a lot of sense."

"None at all, after fourteen years."

"What did you talk about?"

"Our conversation might fill three balloons in a comic strip. He'd been a marine, call him Bobby, I was looking old, he was passing through."

"He didn't ask you for anything, then."

"No."

"Or mention where he was staying."

"He didn't even mention that the FBI would be in later to check on him."

She stood and held out a card. "Please call me if he contacts you again. Where I'm staying is on the back."

I turned it over. The Best Western out by the interstate. Choices being limited hereabouts.

"A warning?" I said.

"Yes?"

"You don't want to eat there."

"Where *do* I want to eat?"

"The café here in town. Only says CAFÉ on the sign, but everybody calls it Happy Bun."

"Noted."

"The Bun shuts down at six. After that your best bet is Bea's Diner. Look for the big yellow smiley face in the window. Eight, ten miles up county road 104 from the motel, past the truck stop."

"Thank you."

"Time was, we'd take a stranger in, feed him. Nowadays we just tell him where to go. So to speak."

We had walked together to the office door. When she turned back to hold out her hand, I shook it. "May I ask where you're based, Agent Ogden?"

"Now we've gone formal. My home office is Richmond."

"Not so far from home after all."

"Geographically, no. But it might as well be another planet."

"And you've traveled all this way. Can you tell me why you're asking about Brandon?"

"I'm sorry."

"Evidently a serious matter, since you've shuffled down here to Willnot."

"It is unusual for us to have so active a role, to be called in. Or so I'm told. You said that Sergeant Lowndes told you he'd been a marine."

"Yes."

"That was incorrect. He still is."

Going out, we all but collided with Maryanne and Cleveland Sims. He had one hand clamped to his face; I flashed on the old story of Tchaikovsky conducting while holding on to his head, convinced it might fall off. With a final good-bye to our friend at the FBI, I ushered Cleveland into exam room one.

Cleveland has the worst TMJ I've seen. Says he lives with a sound like foot soldiers crunching across gravel every time he works his mouth, and every now and again, when he yawns or bites down hard, sometimes even spontaneously, the jaw dislocates. Our routine used to be off to the ER, nurse standing by, IV Valium, wait for the wooze, then hit it. Over the years, with many reps, we've streamlined that to *Ready? Set!* Maybe a world record.

"You got the touch, Doc," he said when we were done. "I'll be looking for that bill, now."

Somewhere between eighty-two and ninety (he wasn't sure himself) and with an annual income in the low three-figure range, Cleveland had never received a bill from me and never would, but we kept up the pretense.

It was growing dark by the time I'd seen the other patients and written everything up, Maryanne long gone. Out my west window an orange sun held on, flattening itself crablike against the horizon to gain a few more moments.

6

SATURDAY. EARLY ROUNDS at the hospital, especially to check in on Mr. Patmore, then, after breakfast back home, *not* the slow-mo weekend day we always hoped for, but sports physicals. Twenty-plus kids from high school who like me would ransom body parts to be doing anything else. There they sat in the waiting room, a salad of T-shirts, shorts, slogans, torn jeans, pressed khakis, tattoos, long hair, no hair, iPads and smartphones, Walkmans, sweat, tobacco smell and cologne.

Weeds, honeysuckle, tall grass, jimsonweed, briar.

I never see this many kids in congress, especially males with their ritual one-liners, posturing and studied indifference, without thinking *Crowds and Power*, adaptation and mimicry, shibboleths, how the gravity of the group pulls one away from center and self. There's a yob inside every one of us, a yob we have to struggle against.

Sometimes I'm able to snag a third-year student from the med school at the capital to come out and help me, but this year it was not to be. The boys and I had only our disgruntled selves. That's a lot of throats to peer into, a multitude of ears, an abundance of abdomens. And even settling for the briefest of histories, a couple of hundred questions. But soldier on we did, and by two in the hastening afternoon our many-legged task was done.

"All that's required is the old bend-and-cough," Richard said. "You could just . . ." He grinned a silly-boy grin—meaning him, or me? "No. You couldn't."

We were in one of our periodic shutdowns, what Richard calls fasting, when news of the world gets held at bay, all the vying for position among politicians, headlines of disasters, hourly updates on wars new and old and unending. The whole parade of foolishness, hunger and pain. I had a simple gauge: if I tear up during commercials, have a catch in my voice when calling about car insurance and meeting not resistance but outright courtesy, I'm in overload.

So for a time we'd watch no TV, read no newspapers, remain reassuringly out of touch. Cultivating our garden. Governments turned outrageous lies, legislation and water cannons against their citizens, cities collapsed as though on time delay into refuse heaps, twelve-year-olds learned the finer points of armed ambush.

And we, Richard and I, were out for a ride. He'd been waiting at home for me to finish with the blockers, sprinters and leapers.

"Interesting how these complaints come up only when I'm a captive audience," I said, "usually in a car."

"Like on, what was it, our second date?"

"Third, maybe. You started going all serious on me—"

"Luckily I've gotten over *that*."

"—and I asked if you were about to inquire what my intentions were."

"Pushy, pushy. Even then."

"Turned out, of course, that you just had the flu."

"Which I freely shared." As we approached the Greenville turnoff, Richard looked to the right. "There she blows."

You always heard the orange VW before you saw it. It had been around forever, passed down, everyone says, from generation to generation. Some claim it's not the same car at all, that a mystery mechanic keeps rebuilding new ones in the image of the original, sneaking in under cover of night and replacing it.

Big Orange has poor brakes, remarkable presence, and implicit right of way, so I slowed as it ran the stop sign. As ever, the driver's hand shot through the sunroof waving wildly.

"Gotta love tradition," Richard said. Moments later he glanced at me. "The sign back there said CAUTION: CHURCH."

One of Richard's great pleasures is misreading signs. Billboards that say FIENDS ARE FOREVER, fence signs announcing that the property is PASTED, warnings to WATCH OUT FOR FALLING CROCKS, that sort of thing. I'm never quite sure if the misreadings are actual or fanciful.

"Yeah, churches are all through here, every half mile or so."

"Like hazardous-material warnings."

"Exactly."

"Don't see many three-story houses in these parts," he said, still looking right, toward a house set well back from the road.

"Actually, if I remember correctly, it was four the last time we came this way."

He made a show of thinking it over. "Good they built it like that, then. Still have three good ones."

"Must be all the rain we've had."

"Sinkage."

"Slippage."

"Defining force of the universe."

He sat quietly, looking out at the trees and soybean fields. Back our first year together, we'd taken a road trip to Galveston. Having seen a bumper sticker that read TECHNICALLY THERE

WOULD ONLY NEED TO BE ONE TIME TRAVELER'S CONVENTION, we stayed on the lookout, and somewhere around Fort Worth, we both saw this license plate:

RVLTN

"Revolution," Richard said.

"You forget what part of the country you're in? More likely Revelation."

We'd stopped for coffee not long after, and as we sat on black cement benches outside the yellow Bzzzy Bee Café, Richard, no doubt still thinking about that license plate, asked me what I really believed in.

We got back in the car, drove on.

"The ability of mankind," I told him, "with tremendous struggle, to be minimally better than its base instincts and inclinations."

7

I HEARD THE code being called as I walked into the hospital that night, to ICU, and felt cold run up my spine.

But it wasn't Mr. Patmore.

Judy Donovan, our nurse practitioner, looked up as I came through the doors. "Respiratory failure. Extubated early this morning." She had it under control, so Gordie and I stood around while she ran the code and reintubated.

"Here to check on your guy from the site?" Gordie asked.

"Yeah. You?"

"Emergency appy. Weintraub called me at home, flushed me away from a perfectly fine martial arts movie."

Minutes later Judy handed me blood gases.

"May want to—"

"Just did. Rate to twelve, dropped the O's and kicked the PEEP up a notch. I'll keep him under till tomorrow morning, see how it looks."

"All shiny, then," Gordie said.

"Thanks, Jude."

"You bet."

Mr. Patmore was fine, watching from his cranked-up bed across the room as the curtains parted and nurses, techs and carts pulled away. Within minutes our night RT, Joseph, was alone at the bedside, securing the ET tube, checking his vent, and setting alarms, getting together paperwork as he waited to draw new gases.

"Guess it can get pretty exciting in here," Mr. Patmore said.

"We keep telling them not to party, but you know how kids are." I looked over the IVs and blood as I stood there. I've been known to be obsessive about such. "How are you feeling?"

"Like someone tied me behind a truck in Omaha and didn't cut me loose till Dallas."

"Any pain?"

He held up the demand button. "I've got my little squeeze-me, don't I?"

"Don't hesitate to use it. We want the pain to come—pain's important, your body talking to you—but we want it to come on slowly. Day or two from now, you'll be okay with that. The rest takes longer. Up to a year for most people to recover from major surgery."

"I'll give it three months."

My kind of patient. I had a momentary urge to hug him, not the best idea with someone who has a freshly stitched abdomen.

An occupied car sat beside mine in the hospital parking lot, a midsize, dun-colored GM. Not a rental, from the look of it and license plate, and not local. The driver ducked his head to watch in the rearview as I came out the ER entrance, followed my progress across weathered asphalt I had trod so many times that it felt as though I were stepping in my own footprints, sinking infinitesimally deeper. His door swung open as I approached. A man of forty or so, well over six feet and so preternaturally thin that his knobby, knotlike joints—elbows, knees, wrists—looked as though they should belong to a much larger man. He'd have passed his childhood being called Ichabod, Spider, Highpockets, or worse. He wore old jeans and a short-sleeve, untucked blue dress shirt. The parking-lot lights gave his skin a yellow cast. An open, active laptop sat on the passenger's seat.

"Doctor Hale? Can we talk?" His attention deflected; he spoke as much to himself as to me. "Why do I keep doing that? Dialog from some crappy script." Waited a beat. "Sorry."

"What is it that I can do for you?"

He held out a hand and we shook. "Joel Stern. I'm with *Loose Leaf*."

"A reporter."

"Yes sir. You know the *Leaf*?"

"I've seen it. But I'm afraid you're off course. I really have nothing to do with the excavation, know less about it, I'm sure, than you do."

"That story would be more for major papers, the networks. We're more like . . . on the edge? Looking in?"

He glanced back into the car as a new page rolled up on his laptop, lingered a moment, wiped.

"Bobby Lowndes, Doctor Hale. He was your patient. I'm here for background on him."

"My question has to be why in the world you'd be wanting background on Bobby. Not that I can say much."

"Perhaps you should."

"The public has a right to know?"

"The public is a great beast, Doctor, far more interested in why some bimbo broke into tears on yesterday's chat show, a politician's most recent 'indiscretions,' or Suzie Q's wardrobe malfunction."

"If you believe that, then why do what you do?"

"I like asking questions. The answers are never as important as the questions."

"Read any Lenin?"

"Ask who benefits, and from whom? Yes sir. Or what science fiction writer Theodore Sturgeon said: Ask the next question."

I flashed on Ted Sturgeon sitting across the coffee table at a party in someone's suite during a convention when I was eight or nine. Sturgeon had this tadpole of a typewriter, so small it looked like a toy, and he was typing away the whole time he talked to me and the party surged around us. Always wondered what it was. He wasn't publishing an awful lot those days.

"It's not from recalcitrance," I told Joel Stern. "I can't say much because there's not much."

I offered the abstract: Bobby's sudden appearance, his sphinx-like remarks, his departure. How he'd stopped out on the street to speak with Old Ezra and given him money.

"Did he know this man?"

"Couldn't have."

"Interesting." Stern glanced again at his computer. Photos were streaming. A desert landscape, an Asian- or African-looking city saturated with off-plumb buildings.

"Have you spoken with an FBI agent by the name of Ogden?"

He nodded. "As you'd expect, on the record she was not forthcoming. Off the record she wanted me to understand, all of this expressed quite politely, that if I got in her way, if I did *anything* to impede her investigation, she'd kick my ass into next Tuesday."

"A free press is so important."

"Everybody knows. So, nothing else you can tell me?"

"Call-me-Bobby that walked into my office is a stranger. And ethics preclude discussing my patient Brandon Lowndes."

"Understood."

We shook hands. He climbed back in his car, shut the top of his computer, then, driver's door still open, swung back around to look up at me.

"Do you know what your old patient did in the service, Doctor Hale?"

"Marines, is all."

"He was a shooter. A scout sniper."

With that, Joel Stern shut the door, fired up an engine that needed work, and pulled away, swimming back into the mainstream, heading for the next edge.

8

"I WAS EIGHT, maybe nine." Our favorite time of day, light slowly fading but not yet forgone, time itself slowing, the moment like a held breath. Wittgenstein: If eternity is timelessness, then eternal life belongs to those who live in the present. "I got home from school and found it on the windowsill outside the kitchen. Hunched back against the glass unmoving, its bright orange kernel of an eye alive with what I recognized as terror. It had been hurt somehow. Damaged. It couldn't fly."

We were sitting outside, a project and mission, or perhaps an altruistic dinner offering, for hordes of mosquitoes who appeared to be quite fond of the smoking candles guaranteed to repel them.

"I kept going out there all afternoon and night, checking up on it. Took food and water out, some dry cat food that it ate. When I went out after dinner, this had to be the fifth or sixth time, it was gone."

"What kind?"

"Magpie, my old man said."

"Cats got it?"

"Cats, dogs, a hawk. Probably so. But in my mind—in my mind, it flew away."

You live with someone year after year, you think you've heard all the stories, but you never have.

Richard slapped at a mosquito on his arm. "Three thousand five hundred species of these wee wonders, and only the females suck blood."

Accustomed as I am to such sidelong pronouncements, I simply smiled.

So that's how it came about, my partner's troth for rescuing animals.

When I was twelve, wholly without prior sign or indication I fell into a coma. My parents came into my room late one morning and found me: not visibly ill, no fever, no rash, breathing slowly and easily, unresponsive. Most of that year I spent in the hospital, my sister at my bedside every possible chance and often allowed by parents and staff to stay overnight, sleeping in a chair by my bed. Katherine was what I first saw when months later, again without prelude, I opened my eyes. She rushed to me and took the hand I vainly attempted to lift. Signals were going out, move, move, but wouldn't catch. Like a battery almost gone, a sparkler that won't stay lit. "What did I miss?" I finally said.

Despite serial EEGs, scans, spinal taps, consultations and conjecture, the doctors never diagnosed the origins of the coma. What we can tell you is just to live, they said. Embrace your life. Don't look back.

Once you've experienced that kind of siege illness, you're forever expecting its return at the first signs of disturbance—indigestion, dizziness, swelling, pain. For years I went to bed anticipating that I might wake up a year later, or never. The thought still drops into my mind late at night sometimes. But such an experience can recut the patterns of your life. Definitely it set me on the path to med school.

What the doctors didn't know, what no one knew, was that I hadn't been alone. The visitors, the others, came to me as I lay there. I don't know when they arrived, the first day, further along, but they were there for most of it. The only world and time I had was theirs.

Before them, there was no blackness, no awareness. Nothing. Then thoughts that seemed fully my own slid into my mind, the memory of walking with an older man along train tracks in woods, and I was opening my eyes, looking around. But my eyes met only blur out there, and I shut them again. As unbearable pain from the burns swept over me.

It could be that my mind, recoiling from the pain, fled that first visitation, but I can't honestly accept that I possessed even so minute a degree of control.

We sat outside a coffee shop, the woman and I, her name was Judith, and I knew, knew without precedent or indication, that she was about to dump me. Many years had passed since them. But as the waiter approached, a great tide of loss swelled within me, as I ordered, as I waited. Her hand reached across the table for mine.

Above me, somewhere near the room's ridged green wall coverings and the silent TV's scrambling cars, words were being mouthed. They were telling me again what happened, how they came home and found me facedown on the floor, that I would be okay. Spanish. And while I don't speak Spanish, I understood every word.

No, not I: the man on the bed.

Again, my eyes opened. I looked up at the light-blue ceiling. Blue, was that the right word? And through the window at a darkening sky. No sense of where I was. Sounds past the door. People talking, phones ringing, heavy objects being moved about. Lifted my hand into light from the hallway. Tube, needle, tape. Thick, ropy blue veins. Faded white line on the third finger where some time ago a ring had been. Hospital armband with a name I, we, don't recognize.

Hundreds of them moved through me as I lay there. First those nearby, other patients, nurses, visitors, staff. Then, gradually, people beyond the hospital walls, out on the street, at the bus stop, across town.

When I woke at the end of that dormant year and my sister, realizing that I was back among the living, stood, I saw myself there on the bed as she drew toward me, I walked with her (right leg stiff and painful from a bike accident) across the floor, I felt the tug of carpet at her shoes, felt the explosion of joy within—felt everything she felt.

And so it would be for some time after. I'd be pouring milk into my coffee mug and with no warning find myself sitting on a riverbank. As I walked by an office high-rise the all-but-unbearable emotional pain of someone within would crash down into me. I lived with double vision: here and not here, I and not-I, I and other. I lived, walked, slept and dreamed in multiple worlds.

Over time it faded, so slowly at first that I took little notice. I was busy, with school, with chores, books, friends. Fishing with my sister. (We called what we did fishing, but mostly this amounted to sitting side by side with poles and tackle box talking.) Till one day—I was in college by then, eighteen or so—I found myself reaching for what was no longer there, understood that I had been doing so, thoughtlessly, for months.

Sometimes even then, in flashes, in stabs, the visitors would come to me, a face, a keen of sadness, shadows. Blades of light sweeping through darkness and quickly gone.

Before the doors shut (I thought) for good.

9

"THE BODIES WEREN'T alone in there," Seb Daiche said, eyes veering to the coffeemaker against the back wall as it began loudly burping. He'd arrived from the site looking like an extra in a safari movie: khaki pants, brown shirt with sleeves rolled above the elbows, brown vest-jacket with multiple pockets. All of it well-worn and well kept. "There was something else under them. Roots, or an ancient cellar, we thought when we first hit. Old wood."

Marcie dealt the plate with my bagel onto the counter and stepped back. Waiting for me to check my cards.

"Anything else?" she said.

Seb asked if tea was possible. Hot? She glanced at him, shook her head, and went to get it.

"Wooden trunks. Two of them, set side by side. Pretty much rotted away, naturally."

"Put there at the same time as the bodies?"

"From all evidence, yes. Almost like a platform. A floor."

"Or Egyptians burying possessions the dead would need in the afterlife," Richard said, and went back to his oatmeal.

"What was in the trunks?"

"Chances are good we'll never know." Seb stopped as Marcie brought a mug of steaming water and a caddy with a dozen or so tea packets. He shuffled through them, pulled out one that smelled faintly of oranges. When he dropped it in to steep, the smell grew strong. Clove in there too.

"The trunks were filled with papers," Seb said.

Richard didn't look up this time, only said, "Not Confederate money as in old movies."

"Just paper. All of it far gone. Whatever the groundwater, worms and insects didn't bleach out or eat away, the chemicals took care of. Our forensics people back in Arizona may find something to latch onto. But if they do, it won't be much."

Having told us what he came for, Seb Daiche knocked back his tea in a single draw and strode out against the incoming wave of breakfast diners.

"Things to do, people to see."

Richard smiled. "Evidently. And I need to be seen at school. But what he said—"

"Which was very little."

"—takes me back. Years and years ago, once when things got really, *really* bad, on the advice of a friend I went to see a Zen master. I tried to talk, to tell him what was going on, out in the world, up in my head, and he stopped me. Sit perfectly still in a room, he said. Do nothing. Think nothing. Sit still in that room for a long time and all possible versions of your self will arise. Realizing they have no reason to stay around, they will depart, leaving behind peace. Peace and your one true self."

"You stood up and walked out."

"Hey . . . that was going to be a good story."

"I may know you too well for stories."

"Stories are all we have, Lamar."

Briefly he touched my hand there on the counter. Our eyes met. My heart paced in its cage.

And one of my possible selves got up off its butt and went to work. Fearlessly into the quotidian.

Specifically a midmorning exploratory laparotomy that turned into a bowel resection, a messy procedure more akin to plumbing or sausage-making than to heroic surgery. Mr. Mayson would be, as Gordie Blythe so eloquently put it, "bagging his goodies for a while," but he'd also be making a full recovery, back to work at his mom-and-pop in three to four weeks.

As I stood there for three-plus hours cutting, stitching, and shooting the bull with fellow sailors, baroque music pumping away in the background, a part of my mind wandered off to Richard's Zen story, and from there to all the years I had wondered why it was that I lived among the broken. My father, mother, their friends, other families of which I caught glimpses—most everyone, it seemed. Till with age it occurred to me that we're all broken, just in different ways. And that the brokenness makes us interesting, makes us who we are.

Ollie Rice was my first patient when I came to Willnot. Huge man who looked as though he could tuck a cow under each arm then go for a leisurely stroll. Along in years but with a full head of hair, albeit it of such a shade of red as to be almost pink, and eyes dark as river stone. He came in, took the chair across my desk. I said something along the lines of what can I help you with and, waiting for response, realized that he was staring past me, over my shoulder.

"The sky is not right. The blue," he said.

I turned to look. Clouds, sketchy trees. Sky.

"Wallpaper," he went on. "I know, I know. Only wallpaper. But still, the blue is wrong."

So I'm thinking Oh dear. But it turns out that Ollie's here not for depression, paranoia, or any of the *DSM*'s three hundred–plus officially diagnosable mental disorders, he's here for gout. Something I can actually help with.

Mentally ill? Who in tarnation (as Richard the schoolmarm would say, were we indeed in the old West) knows? It's a bottomless bag, that term, all kinds of squirmy stuff in there. And Ollie, the town's top mechanic, had worked it out. He'd found purchase and balance. Not really much of a problem that the frame was off plumb.

And a large part of the charm of Willnot.

The place you grow up, the places you live as a kid, you don't give them much thought. Everyone drives a ten-year-old pickup or VW van, well then, that's what people drive. Your house has big honking cattle horns on the front door, you figure everybody does or should or wants to. I'm not sure that as a kid I'd have recognized weird if it walked up and spit in my face. People in Willnot tend to dwell at the thin edge of maps, more than a few of them staring tygers in the eye. Something in their nature that draws them here, keeps them here? Or that seeps in over time from contact? Stand them up against a straight line, they'll lean.

There are no churches in Willnot. A string of them outside the town limits but none within, by ordinance. No Walmart, no chain grocery or pharmacy, discount or big-box stores. No billboards, no street advertising, plain storefronts. "I got on the bus in 2002 and got off it in 1970," Richard says of when he came here.

Over the years as I bounced from place to place, friends complaining that single-handedly I had made a mess of their address books, gradually it occurred to me that no place I'd been came close to Willnot's tolerance for its inhabitants. Not that anyone patently encouraged transgressive or aberrant behavior, but the town refused to isolate exhibitioners thereof, or to hold them in disesteem. With a social equivalent of the Gallic shrug, the town stood back and went on about its business.

Towards noon we got Mr. Mayson squared away in ICU and I defaulted to the office, where Maryanne had five patients corralled. When I mentioned to her that one of the fish was belly-up in the tank, everyone walked over to look.

Routine afternoon. A follow-up for Mrs. Aber who'd broken her hip climbing on a chair to get down a box of mason jars. A teenager with flulike symptoms and, with auscultation, mild rales. What would most likely be just a severely sprained ankle but could be a fracture, so off for X-rays. A newlywed just *sure* she was pregnant. She wasn't. A man brought in by family from Palm Shadows, a retirement home next town over, with what amounted to diaper rash. Last one on the boards was a new patient. I don't get them all that often around here, so they're a pleasure. I love taking H&Ps. It's like reading a biography with all the dull stuff, the dinners and visits from relatives, the bootleg revelations, excised. Kevin Sohl was in his late forties, unmarried, and after living his whole life within a six-mile radius in a "balls-to-the-wall" East Coast city, had picked up of a sudden and put down here. When I asked how it was working out for him so far he said he'd get back to me on that. He didn't have insurance, would pay cash, and wanted to know if that was a problem. Not with anyone I know, I told him.

Time then for Richard's annual nonbirthday party. We had everything set up by seven—hors d'oeuvres on the dining table out front, freshly cut bread, cheese and raw vegetables scattered about, warm food in the oven, wine open and wheezing its slow prime breaths on the kitchen island—with minutes to spare before the first guests arrived. Predictably, Gordie was one of those. Besides a bottle of Scotch that deserved a long gray beard to befit its stature and time on earth, he brought with him a friend visiting from Portland, a physicist who as the evening drew on drank a bit much and began to speak a language no one else understood, English yes, but studded with strange nouns and what seemed a rogue use of verbs, the latter often followed by *of course.*

At one point he and Len Bittner, who teaches philosophy at the state college, stood in a corner of the kitchen together, each speaking his own professional language as the other nodded in wild agreement. Portions I overheard brought home how long it had been since I was in school. How much of what was taught me, how many certainties and core assumptions, now were in question—or discredited?

Richard and I kept ourselves occupied setting out skewers of meat, cutting fresh bread, refilling glasses and trays, wiping spills, scooping up cast-off plates and food. From time to time as feasible, one or the other of us would touch down at some coordinate, a couch, a doorway, a table's edge, to engage in fitful conversation before the tides again took us away.

Around ten, when most of the longhaulers had sunk onto chairs, windowsills or other improvised seats, I went outside. There's an alleyway out back, shored by a stand of oleander across, by thick hedges on our side.

"You could come in, you know."

Bobby Lowndes stepped from behind the garage. "Never much for social situations."

"You've been here a while now. I saw you better than an hour ago."

"I know."

"I could bring you some food. A drink."

Lights went on behind the oleanders. Bobby turned his head that way. "You didn't tell me your sister died in Afghanistan," he said.

"It's not something I talk about."

Bobby looked up. "Getting crisp. Winds about six mph now, but there's a push behind. Those clouds'll have heavy bellies come morning."

He looked down the alley. In the dark, this isolated path could be the whole world.

"The only thing that keeps civilization from flying apart, Doc? Specialized knowledge. How to build a fire, skin a rabbit, find water, set bones, figure taxes. Bullets move about three inches for every mph of wind speed. You back off focus in your spotting scope, and you don't look at the site but at the mirage, the heat waves. The angle of their rise gives you your wind speed."

I made no response. Bobby watched a car go by on Maple Street a block away. The driver was alternately gassing it and hitting the brake, so that the car bucked slowly along, hiccuping into view from the west hedges and out of sight again past Paul Baumann's storage shed. What fun.

"You remember why you got to be what you are, Doc? Where that started?"

"It's a long story."

"Most are." I watched him hear something, tilt an ear that way, discount it. "Like all those stories about people coming back from death. That's what you and I did."

How he could know about that, I had no idea. Or about my sister. Neither was information I freely shared.

"We weren't dead."

59

"Who's to say?"

He turned and walked down the alley, moving at what seemed a relaxed pace yet covering ground rapidly. At the street he waved and was gone. Up that way, at the old Haversham place, lights went off, then on again. New people over there. Richard and I hadn't met them yet.

Then I felt it, just as I'd felt it back in the hospital when I came around and saw my sister moving toward me, just as I'd experienced it during those silent, still months. Another world, another mind, coming into my own.

Again. After all these years.

I lay in bed, sheets in damp whorls about me. Weak greenish light from the aquarium across the room. Continuous soft exhale of a humidifier. Sweet, pungent smell of my body. My daughter slides close on the chair, puts her hand gently on the parchment skin of my arm, tells me that I have to rest, to get some sleep. That she'll be right here with me.

I can't. I can't sleep. If I close my eyes, that's the end.

10

A RECURRENT FANTASY from childhood, before the coma, I think: That the world was rebuilt each time I slept. Sure that if I listened hard in the darkness I'd be able to hear carpenters at work, masons grunting as they hoisted stone, the stage manager creaking up ladder steps to hang the moon or sun.

I woke the next morning to the indescribable sound of Richard in the shower singing about *things we've left behind*. Steam was so thick in the bathroom, I'd have tested out just then as legally blind. As it cleared with the open door I saw the little misshapen heart he'd drawn on the mirror, with my initials beneath.

I tapped on the shower door. "A bit of empathy here, please. *Things left behind* has special meaning to someone who does surgery for a living."

"What? Like bills? Remortgaged homes?"

"Like sponges. Clamps."

"Rather than fond memories. I see your point. Could take the fun right out of catheters, suppositories and head-banging drugs. But then, no vacation is perfect." He pulled the door back. "Join me?"

"Depends. Is the singing done?"

"I sing when I'm lonely."

I got in.

By early afternoon, I was out at the Farrels' drinking watery coffee at the kitchen table. I'd done rounds (Mr. Mayson of the bowel resection coming along fine, Betty Evans ready to go home sans gallbladder, and Gar Billstrup whose seizures were a puzzle—awaiting test results from University Hospital) and I'd doddered around the empty office for an hour or so, then grabbed the phone and asked Maryanne to call me if.

For someone so well-nigh compulsive about my professional life, Richard says, I'm a champ at putting off personal matters.

So there I sat, attending to one such.

Sort of.

"I know we're late with the rent," Sis said. She was the older of two daughters. Everyone called her that. "What, four months? Or I guess five by now."

I asked where everyone was.

"Susan's back with Don. Daddy got some day work over at the Johnsons', helping fix their roof."

"And Carol Anne?" Their mother.

"Oh, she took off, must have been most of a year ago. You didn't know?"

"I saw Don in April. Your father never said anything."

"Pride." She poured more coffee without asking. The chocolate-chip cookies sat staring up at me. There were always chocolate-chip cookies. Don loved them. He'd leave them in his mouth awhile then spit them out.

To my knowledge Don was the only Farrel, before Carol Anne anyhow, ever to leave camp. He'd wandered in small steps toward the city, where somehow or other he got entangled in dealing coke, pills and who knows what. Did pretty well, till the day his rivals drove up, grabbed him, and threw him headfirst over a wall. Boy was tough, though, thousands of years of hard-ass Scots-Irish stock, so here he was, paralyzed from the neck down, recovered from multiple bouts of pneumonia and infection, still with us. Mornings they'd bathe and dress him, faithfully keep him turned every hour or so. Fingers splayed on pillows, displaying the gold-nugget, dollar-sign and death's-head rings he'd worn back in that other world.

"Don's okay?"

"He's fine. Go say hi, Doctor Hale. Susan's just reading to him."

"I better get back to the office. Tell him hi for me."

"Take some cookies with you?"

I waited as she found a plastic bag, clean but clouded from reuse, and filled it. Thanked her, told her I'd be looking forward to the cookies and not to worry about the rent, we'd settle up later.

I had just turned off the dirt road onto the highway when the phone rang. I'd been perfectly content with the ring my phone acquired at birth, but Richard had taken it and installed the opening bars of Fats Waller's "Your Feet's Too Big." Any complaint, he told me, and there would be vanity license plates and monogrammed sweaters in my future. Ooh, I said. Aaah.

I pulled over, flipped the phone open, but didn't get Maryanne as expected.

"Sorry to bother you, Dr. Hale. This is Janet. I'm in charge today and in ER. There's a woman here named Theodora Ogden. She asked that I call you. Says you know a Bobby or Brandon Lowndes—"

"I do."

"He's been shot."

. . .

I stepped through the door and saw the top of Chester Wilde's bald head with the bright lights bouncing off it. Chet to friends, Doc Savage to others, Doc had retired a decade ago but every few weeks couldn't stand it any longer, brought in coffee for the ER staff, and hung around. He'd been there when they rolled Bobby through the doors, set down his cup without a word, and stepped up. Doc's a kind you don't see anymore, who could do a clean resection or bypass with a steak knife and a couple of C-clamps.

I'm forever amazed at how sloppy ER workers are—as though the presumed urgency of their ministrations gives them license. Same tools, much the same procedures as upstairs in OR. There, we place our packaging, detritus and bloody sponges in bins. Here, often as not, everything gets tossed on the floor. Guy comes in with a stab wound or sprained ankle, the place looks like a war zone by the time he ships out.

From the doorway I nodded to the nurses. "Bent over your work again, eh, Doc?"

"This back of mine, I'm bent over every gottdam thing. What are you waiting for—get over here."

"Nowadays we tend to wash our hands first."

"Youngsters and your newfangled ways. Go ahead, then, take your time. This boy ain't gonna die anytime soon, with or without you."

He had the bleeding stopped, I saw when I drew up bedside. Fluids going in for volume. Cleaning the wound of debris. Swabbing. Probing. Vitals good.

"That is one puny-looking GSW."

"Shooter thought he was after squirrel maybe," Doc said.

"Twenty-two?"

"Low caliber anyway. Round's over there."

"Who the hell shoots a man with a pea?"

Doc straightened. As close to straight as he gets. Looked like his glasses hadn't been wiped since about 2000. "Someone who's real good, would be my guess."

Soon after, the OR crew showed up to transport, Gordie Blythe with them. Doc reported off, and I went out to where Agent Ogden waited, lavender blouse bright among dun-colored chairs and walls, head-to-head with her smartphone. She finished what she was about before closing the app and standing.

"That conversation couldn't have gone well," I said.

"It wasn't much of a conversation. How is he?"

I heard her phone buzzing softly in the pocket of her suit coat. I waited. She didn't answer.

"From what I saw in there, he's been through a hell of a lot worse."

Just then the automatic doors swung open, X-ray attendants bringing a patient back to ER, masthead of IV bags, body mummy-wrapped, oxygen cylinder like a small missile alongside in the bed. We looked up, a response as automatic as the doors, and saw Joel Stern standing by the wall. He'd pulled a second, flannel shirt over the one he wore when we met out in the parking lot four days back. The shirt's long tails made him look even taller and thinner. And it hadn't been the parking-lot lights that gave his skin that yellow cast.

"Sorry about the eavesdropping," he said. "Professional habit."

From Joel Stern, who had been half a block away, closing in on Bobby after pinballing behind him all over town, I learned that the shot was barely audible, recollected only afterward upon seeing Bobby fall, a light pop or crack, Joel said, like a stick breaking underfoot. Joel had placed the 911 call and done what he could by way of first aid.

From Andrew, whom I found in the cafeteria eating a slice of pie that overlapped its plate the way a fat man's midriff overlaps his belt, I learned a little more.

"Good pie, huh?"

"Always." He was using a spoon.

"You brought in a gunshot a while back."

"The soldier? Uh-huh."

"How did you know that?"

"Heard talking."

"The ER crew?"

"Uh-huh." Another bite of pie went away.

"Was he conscious?"

"By the numbers he was. But he just looked at me. Like . . ."

I waited.

"Like he was flat. Somebody let the air out?"

"What did the soldier have with him?"

Andrew's quirks kicked in. "Shirt, dark blue, size sixteen—we cut that off. Khaki pants, almost new, thirty-six waist, thirty-two length. New Balance walking shoes, elevens, maroon and gray. Cream-colored baseball cap, no writing."

"Was there anything else? A backpack? A weapon?"

"He had a wallet with an Oregon driver's license, a Visa card expiring in July, sixty-seven dollars. Fifty-eight cents in change in his left pocket. No belt."

"And did he say anything? Try to?"

"Only at first, when he first looked up at me. Sounded like 'Billygoat, that you?'"

"'Billygoat, that you?'"

"Like that. Twice."

11

NEXT MORNING WE watched the parade as Sebastian Daiche's pit team pulled out, vehicles shedding gravel and dirt as they trooped down Maple Street toward the interstate. Felt like when you're a kid standing at the edge of town seeing the carnival leave. Bye-bye, mystery and magic. Hello, ordinary life.

Not that it was.

Gordie and I were sitting on one of the benches out front, drinking bad coffee as people came and went through the hospital's front entrance.

Strange how you can work alongside someone for years, have him as a friend, then one day suddenly understand—not simply know, but understand—that his beliefs are so unlike what you thought. That he lives in quite a different world from the one you had him in.

Strange too how we'd failed to get the press attention we expected. Two skeleton news crews had straggled in, but for the most part interest in Willnot's "shocking find" had been eclipsed first by the latest Washington scandal, then by eruption of new civil wars in another small part of this large, unwieldy world.

My chief back during residency, Teddy Wu, kept telling us that life is just a long recovery before the fatal illness strikes. Bobby Lowndes lay inside in ICU recovering—from what, besides a bullet wound? I'd been brought up around people with a profound mistrust of received wisdom, appearance, surfaces. My father used to quote André Gide: "Fish die belly upward and rise to the surface. It's their way of falling." His old friend Ted Sturgeon said always ask the next question.

And the next question here was who shot Bobby? And why?

The same people who'd fostered in me such skepticism for received wisdom, for what we all know, steadfastly mistrusted the government. Talk of CIA assassinations, the coup in Chile, illegal wiretaps and entrapment flowed about me the way other children grew up hearing about the latest TV shows, hometown football team, or summer vacation. I didn't hesitate to question whether Bobby's own agency and bureaucracy might have acted against him.

"You think much about government conspiracies?" I asked my benchmate, provoking two quick volleys of laughter that turned heads toward us.

"You're seriously asking this of someone who chooses to live in Willnot? Government *is* conspiracy. We all know that."

It wasn't what he said so much as it was the pressure behind it. My old friend, staid, lightly comedic Gordie with his tailored suits and country-club membership up at the capital, had been flying under false colors all these years?

He laughed again. "When I was twelve, a friend of my father who was a movie nut proudly brought over a print of *Invaders from Mars* and a projector to show it, real old-school. The boy in that movie saw something no one else did. That Others were here, picking us off one by one. People would be walking along and the ground would give way beneath them, swallow them up."

"*Yeah,* I thought.

"And from that moment on—I even remember the taste of the lemon drops I was sucking on, and the bristly fabric of the couch—I've never been far from awareness that the depths are there, with the thinnest of membranes covering them. Any moment, the membrane can give."

"This from someone who puts people to sleep for a living."

"Most of them wake up."

He shifted on the bench as his pager went off. "Nothing is *ever* what it seems. A realist is someone who thinks the world is simple enough to be understood. It isn't." The beeper went off again as he was checking it. "In my head I was the kid, of course, right up there on the screen, in the movie. When I saw it again years later, I had to wonder if, consciously or not, the adults didn't know the kid was right. That if they admitted it, the world would unravel around them."

Gordie stood. "And Bo Sanders may unravel if I don't get up there. Wouldn't put it past the new kid surgeon—the one that looks like, I don't know, fourteen with a bullet? and so, so eager?—to start cutting on poor Bo without me."

I went in for one last graze before heading officeward. Bobby remained sedated, but vitals were good and the lab work, given the circumstances, was well within bounds, no cause for concern.

Sheriff Hobbes sat outside the room, covering for a deputy who was seeing to a traffic accident. He stood to poke at the cushion on the chair as I approached. "Damn thing's got Sam's buttprint stamped in here for good." He told me that Agent Ogden had taken herself off to the crime scene (meaningful pause here) again. I called Maryanne to say I'd be in soon and swung over to that side of town.

I knew the house. Seth Addison was likely the oldest person in these parts, around when the town started up. After he died, the house went empty save for frequent break-ins inspired by rural legend that Seth never had any use for banks, that all the money he'd made in his ninety-plus years on earth was hidden there.

Overgrown railroad tracks lead you to a patch of rusted, ancient farm machinery and from there up a rut-bedeviled hill to what's left of the house, sheets of plywood bowing away from doors and windows over which they had been nailed. Along one side are scars where decades ago a balcony got torn away. One side droops as though the house suffered a stroke.

Theodora Ogden sat at a thirty-degree tilt on the lowest porch step picking splinters out of her butt.

"Old wood," I said. "Musician friends tell me it's the best."

"Sure they do."

"If that's evidence . . ."

"Only of my stupidity. I hope you're not here because—"

"Bobby's fine. Should be awake and vocal by early afternoon. What are you looking for? Surely the scene's been gone over."

"Inspiration, maybe."

"And all you found was rotting wood."

"Well, it is quiet out here."

"Quiet's a thing we've got our share of."

"I turned the cell phone off, drove out. No real agenda, and I didn't think there'd be anything to see. Maybe just needed quiet."

"Or to be alone."

"Alone is good."

"I could leave . . ."

She motioned to the step beside her and I sat, saying that chances were good we'd have to desplinter one another when we were done, but I was a doctor, after all, so she needn't be shy.

"Alone scares people," I said. "A lot of them."

"My mother always had the TV on, early morning, late at night, during meals. Rarely looked at it, couldn't have told you what show was on, but there it was, this visitor that never left."

"People need the space around them filled. It's the pressure." A cat came from under the house, looked at us without curiosity, and went on its way. "You know what my father did."

"Of course."

"I can't tell you how many scenes I read as a kid where some guy ruptures his spacesuit or his ship and gets sucked out, horribly but at considerable length and with excellent description, into the vacuum. It's like that—your mother's TV, sounds, possessions, the press of others."

The cat sat at yard's edge watching us. Maybe we were prospective buyers and soon there'd be companionship, comforting sounds above. Food.

"No one saw the shooter. The round had some distance to it. That and the caliber rule out an amateur. Yet except for blood loss, Sergeant Lowndes is all right. And who around here has any reason to shoot him?"

"Why does the shooter have to be from around here? Though, mind you, pretty much everybody who is, knows guns."

She stood. "None of it makes any sense."

"Does it have to?"

"Things usually do."

"Only if you're an accountant." Or paranoid—in which case everything connects. "How are you doing with those splinters?"

"I think I can manage."

"Then I should be getting back to the office."

Clouds were gathering as I drove—gathering surreptitiously.

Sky would be clear above a stand of trees, I'd look back and clouds had claimed squatter's rights.

Her mother's TV, the visitor who never leaves, and loneliness . . .

Later in life my hardcore-SF father turned to fantasy. His last novel was *Dying with Grace*, Grace being a two-foot-tall giraffe who wandered up to the protagonist's side one day on the streets of Brooklyn and never left. From that day he was never alone, even in his final moments. The last thing he saw was Grace's face bending over him. She had to stand in a chair to do so.

12

I LOST A patient that afternoon. I'd barely got back to the office and was looking over the first chart when Maryanne came into the examining room to tell me they needed me at the hospital. I arrived to find Gordie, two nurses and his teenage surgeon bent over a gurney like birds at a watering hole. When one straightened and stepped away for a moment, I saw who the patient was. Burt Feldman.

Fifty-three years old, at least forty of those years given over to fighting or, more correctly, surrendering to diabetes. He'd gone blind long ago, had such severe neuropathy that he hadn't walked more than a dozen steps at a time in a decade, his legs were half-and-half sores and necrotic tissue.

And now, from all appearances, he was in DIC, covered with bruises and hemorrhaging from mouth, nose, ears, eyes.

"Sepsis, we figure," Gordie said without looking up. He had Burt on a vent, had his jaw pulled down peering into his mouth. "Clots everywhere. Lucky I was able to get the tube in. Looks like black granola in here."

"Kidneys are gone," the surgeon said.

Janet, one of the new nurses, looked up from the chart. "There's no DNR."

"He's Doctor Hale's patient," Gordie said.

"Sorry. Didn't know."

"How long?"

Janet glanced at the clock. "Forty-six minutes. A deliveryman saw him lying in his front yard, called it in. Unconscious and unresponsive to pain but still breathing when he got there, Andrew says."

I looked up at the skittery, slowing EKG.

"Mostly just the drugs," Gordie said.

"Is there anyone we should notify?" Janet asked.

"He doesn't have family." I looked down at the bruised chest, taped lines, distended stomach. "If it's okay with everyone, I'm going to ask that we leave Burt in peace now. I'll sit here with him."

They filed out, pulling the curtain around us for privacy.

It didn't take long. Twelve minutes maybe. Holding his hand, purposefully not watching the monitors whose alarms I had shut off, I could feel when the moment came. I remembered how much Burt loved *Gunsmoke*, and I was talking to him about that, trying to recall bits and pieces I'd seen of the show over the years, when he died.

Upstairs, Bobby was adamantly stable, his room museum-quiet, though anesthesia and sedation had to have been flushed from his system hours before. Clayton was there changing a dressing and hanging a fresh IV. A Gulf War vet, Clay stands five feet six inches and weighs in at 160, the bulk of it hard flesh and muscle. A trucker in ER once made some smart-ass comment about male nurses and suddenly found one's face looming like a thundercloud four inches above his own.

74

Clay looked up as I came in. "Man's been in country."

"More than a few times, from what I hear."

"So he comes home and gets shot here in Willnot? That's not even irony, that's some other kind of horse entirely."

I nodded.

"We had this platoon leader back on the sand who was always telling us the cards get dealt facedown, you don't ever know what they are till you turn them over. He said that again right before he got shot clean through the head from damn near two thousand yards by a sniper. I'm done here, Doc. You need anything?"

"Just dropped by to check on Bobby."

"I heard you took care of him when he was a kid."

"That was a long time back. Different lives now."

"For all of us."

Clay left and I stood by Bobby. Where was he? Dreaming of rice fields, acres of sand, bright tropical birds shifting on their perches, the smell of hot metal, the burn of mescal on his tongue? I took a last look at the monitors and started out, hearing behind me:

"It appears I've been sleeping again."

As I turned back, Bobby sat up. Heart rate and blood pressure rose when he did so. For moments then he was quiet, breathing slowly, deeply. I watched heart rate and BP fall on the monitors.

"You've been awake."

"A while." He blinked. "Vision's blurry."

"And?"

"Back on familiar ground. Getting shot, losing a chunk of time. Kind of where I live."

He swung his legs experimentally off the side of the bed.

"Need help?"

He shook his head. "Wanted to tell you. I read one of your old man's books. In Iraq, maybe Afghanistan. Cities, towns,

America—everything we knew—couldn't have been farther away. Like we'd been set down on another world and would never get back there, or maybe *there* was gone. Your father's book was about a planet of sand and phantoms. He was writing about someplace else exactly the way we were living it. That book got passed from hand to hand till it fell apart. And then it got taped back together.

"A guy from Earth, Mack or Rutger, some manly name, has just arrived on this world he knows nothing about to fix everything for those who live there. Witnessing what appears to be a senseless, purposeless suicide, he says 'We do not speak ill of the dead.'

"His guide starts to respond, stops to thump on the fritzing translator box to get it to work, then says 'Here, we do not speak of the dead at all, else they believe you are calling them back, and return.'"

"Missed that one."

He twisted in a hard spiral right, then left. "Feels like someone took a sledgehammer to my shoulder—which pales beside the screaming headache. But most of all, I'm just fucking thirsty."

I poured water for him, told him to take it slow.

"In combat, you get hit, you go down. Wait to see what's coming next. Same thing." He drank the full cup. "There wasn't a second shot. Everything still works. And here I am talking to you. Fully confident that the local cop stationed outside my door is there only to protect me from further harm."

"State police, actually."

"Let me guess. Per request of our buoyant friend from the FBI."

"Buoyant?"

"She keeps bouncing up."

"Get some rest, we'll talk later. Pain meds are ordered."

"Won't need them."

"You can refuse."

"That's how I got here in the first place, refusing."

I waited but he added no more.

"Doc?"

I turned back at the door.

"No worries. That shot? Just an old friend's way of saying hello."

Head down, eyes up: a classic gleek from Maryanne as I came in the door. "Two walked, two waiting, one pledged to come back later."

Not a bad tally, considering.

"I thought about holding his driver's license, tell him he could redeem it when he returned."

"Are we that desperate?"

"Not yet. Freda Malone's in your office."

"Is Michael—"

"With her."

And his head was already turning toward my voice when I walked in. Freda held him up.

"See how much weight he's put on!"

Michael had become my occasional patient at age eleven months, having begun life four months early at just over a pound. Now he was three. He'd spent five months in the NICU at University Hospital and still went there for major problems or checkups; between times, he came to see me. *See* being a metaphor only, since he'd lost his eyesight to oxygen toxicity. But he knew my voice, always turned toward me when he heard it.

I said hello to Freda and asked if Michael was all right. She said again "See how much weight he's put on!" and started crying. I sat down in the chair by her and took the boy.

"He's fine," she sputtered.

"And you're not."

She held her breath a moment to still the tears. "Michael's daddy, he left us, been two weeks ago Tuesday."

Michael's daddy. Not Preston, or Pres.

It's something you see a lot with chronically ill children. No matter how close the couple is, how devoted, the demands eat away at families. So much of the caretaker's time and energy is spent on the child that there's little left over for husband or wife, other kids, any pretense of a normal life. Ties wither. Affection fades. Tamped-down anger on every side.

"What did Preston say?" I asked.

"You know him, three words would be a speech."

And communication's the first thing to go. Not that Preston was much of a talker to start with. More a nod-for-hello, grunt-to-indicate-he-was-listening kind of guy.

"He left a bunch of money, said he'd send more."

"Have you talked to your social worker about this? Cathy, is it?"

"You mean Candy up at the hospital, that's been following Michael? No."

"Do. She can talk you through this. Ask her to call me if there's anything I can help with."

Michael had to be among the quietest babies ever, always attentive, always reactive, but rarely emitting sounds. As though his beginnings, as he lay intubated and unable to cry or vocalize, subject to continuous pain and discomfort, had set silence indelibly at the center of his world.

I held out a finger, he nibbled at it, I handed him back to his mother.

"You know you can call me anytime, right?"

"Thank you. I'm . . . I'm really scared. Not like before, not even all those times Michael was doing so poorly. This is different."

I walked Freda to the door and asked Maryanne to give me a minute before sending anyone in. I'd almost told Freda "You'll be fine" but stopped myself. All those phrases that sprout so easily on the tongue, the dross of bad movies and hospital corridors: *It will get better, It's for the best, Everything will be okay, You'll be fine.* I had promised myself during residency to delete them from my vocabulary. Yet another promise I hadn't kept, perhaps couldn't keep, but I hung close.

It wouldn't get better for Freda, or would do so by tiny, invisible increments. She would never be fine. She would never *see* fine, never so much as catch sight of it on a hilltop far away, beckoning.

13

"THE ASSIGNMENT WAS to write about where you live, at least three pages. The idea being, what we talked about in class before, that most of us are forever looking off into the distance, don't see the world around us. Nathan turned in twenty-three pages. With a note apologizing and saying he knew how busy I was and I didn't have to read all of it."

"This is the ant-farm kid, right?"

"Ant mill. But yes."

Richard was in his homeboy clothes, baggy tan pants, unbuttoned plaid shirt over a T-shirt the legend of which had long faded away but which I knew to be WONDER DOG. Dressed for school he'd be in pressed slacks, shirt and tie. Here at home he looked as if he might be on his way to a grunge-band rehearsal.

"He went back to America's beginnings, to the utopian communities: Oneida, New Harmony, Brook Farm. All those struggles to create one small part of the world that was better. By example, by exemption. Nathan suggests that there's something there, something in our blood as Americans, that we never got away from. Then he moves closer on the timeline. Listen.

"'My grandfather says how during World War II everybody thought what they were doing would change the world for good, that when it was over they would come up for air into this peaceful, fair and free society. But that instead, things went back to how they were before. Women who had worked hard jobs in factories and held everything together got hustled back to their kitchens. All the ideals that had seen soldiers and civilians through it got pushed aside, forgotten. The new goal: produce, own, produce more, own more. Consume.'

"Then he flashes forward to the sixties. How the peace movement, the youth movement, thought they'd change the world with their music, their freedom, their new communalism. And he quotes a contemporary Marxist historian: 'America did again what it always does. It absorbed the discord, turned it soft; bottled the rebellion and poured in water till it was potable, till it was safe.'

"The world could never be like that, of course, the way communalists envisioned. Nathan knows it. But he keeps asking why we still carry that image in our minds. And all the time he really *is* writing about where he lives, about Willnot."

"The way it started, at least."

"There's still a lot of smoke from that old fire."

"And lost causes never really are—someone always finds them again?"

Richard picked up a handful of papers from beside the computer, held them toward me as though, having heard the abridged version, I'd now have no choice but to read it in full.

"He turned this in on paper?" I said. "All twenty-three pages?"

"I printed it out. So it wouldn't get wiped once the semester's over. It's old hat to us, Lamar. But not for a twelve-year-old. Think about it. His sense of history, of how events aren't isolated.

The connections he makes. What made this kid think his way through all this in the first place? Twelve years old and he's asking questions like this, seeing things so differently? What's going to happen to him? How's he going to survive?"

"We did."

Richard looked toward the doorway, where Dickens sat licking his lips. "We did, didn't we? And so did Dickens, who really, *really* needs food now."

I followed them out to the kitchen, fetching a small can from the pantry and handing it over.

"I went with my father once to see Damon Knight and Kate Wilhelm at their house in Milford," I said. "A long bus ride from Port Authority, and you asked the driver to let you out just outside town, at the foot of a hill. Up above was this looming structure that looked like where the Addams Family could have lived. Damon had a welcome mat that said GO AWAY. Immediately upon returning home I copied that, lettering and all, as a sign for the door to my bedroom."

Richard laughed. "I'd have had no need for it, having spent my childhood alone in my room."

He spooned savory food, beef and gravy smells, into the red bowl that had been his as an infant and now belonged to Dickens.

"I had parent-teacher conferences today, probably why I'm thinking so hard about Nathan. So much came back to me. How my own parents had no friends, least of all one another. How when they rarely spoke it was 'What's for dinner?' or about things that had happened long in their past. There was nothing left, nothing between them, but ritual."

Putting the bowl down, he said, "In my dreams I'm still always alone."

I went to him. "But not here."

"No, not here."

Dickens looked up briefly and went back to eating.

"Lamar."

I sat up. "What?"

Dickens crouched at the end of the bed, eyes huge, ears flattened.

"You've been dreaming. And for two or three minutes shouting in what sounded like Polish or Russian."

"Saying what?"

"You missed the part where I said it wasn't English? Some kind of negotiation, from the sound of it. Trying to convince someone of something. Or reason with them."

I lay back. The pillow was soaked with sweat, and cold. Dickens said "Prrrup?"

Random images swirled back into my mind, sensations, bits of connective tissue. It hadn't been a dream, but a habitation. A visitor.

Pale green light somewhere across the room. Damp-animal smell of a humidifier whose filter badly needed changing. A hand on my arm, and when I looked down it was like a catcher's mitt holding a stick. Not much left of me.

Something I had to do.

"Ruby Jo . . ." Where the fuck had we got that name? Ruby Josephine. What a load to drop on a little girl's shoulders.

"I'm here, Dad."

And here was . . .? Right. Back at the old house. I remembered watching Compton Street roll by the van's windows, where you'd never know sixty years had passed, then brighter lights as we hit downtown, which you'd still miss if you blinked. The house had seen dozens of souls since, the town had known hundreds, but both felt like an old sweater you found in the back of the closet. When you tried it on, it still fit.

We'd talked a lot about our heritage back then, about keeping things in perspective, opting out of bigger, better, faster. About how the country started, or how we believed it had. Benny'd been so fond of the word *should* that we finally had to make him stop using it. Fined him $10 every time it came up. Benny's money in our pockets, stars in our eyes, and not much else. What did we know? We were kids. Belief, though—that was the other thing we had. Poor sons of bitches.

"Can I get you anything?"

You sure can, Sweetheart. And it's a long list, 'cause that's where everything I had has gone, it's all on that list. You can get me being able to swing my wasted legs out of this bed and walk. Get me being able to eat real food. Not have to pee every thirty minutes or wear these fucking diapers. You can get me being able to do what I have to do.

"Dad, it doesn't matter. Not after all these years."

She isn't a little girl any longer, of course. I look up, there's this old woman sitting there. My girl, my Jo still, but an old woman. Seems wrong.

Like so much else.

"No one remembers. No one cares, or thinks about it. We've talked about this, Dad."

And we have, again and again. Yet here, spitting in the face of all good sense or practicality and against your every protest, we are. Here in the old house. Here in the town that was going to repave one of the world's streets, reinvent virtue, save the few from the many.

Like all those end-of-the-world stories, spaceships loaded with travelers off to begin civilization afresh elsewhere, Benny would say. *Did* say. Till we had to start fining him for that too.

No one meant anything by it at first, I can't even remember how it got started. Someone saying *You know* . . . , somebody else coming in with *And the thing is* . . . Then before you know it we're all spinning out, trying to top one another, it's become this super-weird cutting session, the world according to could-be.

Richard's hand was on my chest. "You went back to sleep."

"I . . ."

He waited. Dickens thwapped my leg with his tail. "Anything I can do?"

"You're here."

"So it would seem."

Moonlight lay lazily on the floor, depthless as clouds moved into place, bright and brimming as they passed.

"Then I'm good."

Dickens arched his back and threw up. Too much schmaltz, obviously.

14

"AND THIS IS what?"

"Norm Posner's stool sample."

"In a PEZ container."

"Not to worry, he says, it's been boiled."

"And duct-taped shut." The tape cut in half lengthwise, with dull scissors, probably; six or seven fibers jutted whiskerlike from the cut. "We didn't give him a specimen jar?"

"Says Dolly used it for something else."

I made a collection note in Norm's file on the computer. "Will the lab accept it like this?"

"We can try. Maybe they'll be having a slow day. I'll mark it urgent, see if that helps."

Eight years of study and here I am staring at shit in a candy tube. Wouldn't take much force to bend that into a metaphor. "Alimentary, my dear," Richard said when I told him about it.

Maryanne was back in the door almost before she left.

"They need you in OR. Vinny says Dr. Mawby's about to kill someone."

Vinny, a self-taught accountant with no medical background

whatsoever but a ferretlike nose for finances, had been acting administrator for seven or eight years. He'd been appointed pro tem after the death of old Doc Storm, and consonant with Willnot's general notion that going with things as they are is better than messing with them, Vinny just never got up out of the chair.

Jules Mawby, on the other hand, was Chet Wilde's dark twin. Chet had retired but couldn't stay away from patients and kept visiting ER; Mawby no longer had any business being near a patient but wouldn't pack it in. Granted, that was all he had. Years back, on the way home from a trip to Disneyland, his wife, son, daughter-in-law and grandchildren had died in a car accident. Six people tired, laughing, gone. We'd seen the shakes move into his hands, the unsteadiness as he made his way down the halls, the times he'd step away somewhere inside himself, still and unresponsive, then dial back in.

I found him drinking coffee in the nurses' lounge. He always preferred it to the larger doctors' lounge, said it had a warmth and sense of comfort ours lacked. I poured a cup for myself and sat beside him. I could smell the mouthwash and the odor of his body, metabolism transfigured by alcohol.

"Vincent told me you were coming," he said.

"I guess you know why."

He nodded. "Been a while since we saw one another, Lamar. How's Richard?"

"He's good."

We sat listening to food carts grumble off elevators out in the hall. Two nurses came in talking quietly and, seeing us, withdrew.

"This can't go on, Jules. You know that."

"I know." He finished his coffee in two swallows. "You're catching this one for me?"

"That's why I'm here."

"Nothing to it. Simple nip-and-tuck."

An inguinal hernia that had, as they sometimes do, gone ambitious.

He washed his cup at the sink, rinsed, washed again, and hung it back on the pegboard.

"I do know, Lamar," he said.

Six days later a neighbor went over and, getting no response, called the police. Water for a recently planted Chinese elm had been left on, turned the backyard into a pond. Jules Mawby lay atop a freshly made bed in his own pond of piss, vomit and feces, bottles of Seconal, Darvon and oxazepam like sentinels at bedside. Lined in a precise row on the kitchen counter were bottles of bourbon and Scotch; apparently he'd poured the contents down the sink.

We should have got help for him. We should have stopped him, not let him go on practicing, not covered for him. Someone should have befriended the man. I should have checked on him.

Shoulds will take you off at the knees.

In my dream, people have begun wearing their bones outside their skin. I'm interviewing them to try to understand how they do this, how they learned.

First you have to step away from knowing it's not possible, one adept tells me.

Then with the next foot you step outside your self, another says.

The second adept looks suspiciously like Richard.

Outside my dream, life drifts on, turning slowly in the current, banking lazily off the shore, and the usual workaday miracles keep step beside us.

That morning, with the office empty and all the ambition of a walnut, I stood at the window. Down at the corner Ezra sat on a chewed-up, discolored Styrofoam cooler, not quite on Maple, not quite on Mulberry. I remembered Bobby giving him money that first day back. Our lives are so ungraspable. Turn them one way and light glints off them; turn them another, they drink up the light wanting more. We go to ground believing we're heading one place and come up someplace else entirely.

Jules Mawby.

Ezra.

Bobby Lowndes.

Me.

My second year into residency I pulled most of my hours at the county hospital, 819 beds filled with those who lived in the invisible city, people not just marginalized but off the page entirely. Critically ill newborns abandoned by parents who had moved away when police went to their addresses. Forty-year-old men who looked eighty and survived off saltine crackers and beer. Children with melonlike bellies, bones as flexible as rubber horseshoes, and skin resembling plastic wrap. One day, changing the dressing on a stab wound, I'd asked a twelve-year-old named Louie what he wanted to be when he grew up and he said "Alive."

"Among ourselves we call it landing," Bobby told me later that day.

He'd been moved to a room with a window, outside which the head and shoulders of the trooper on duty showed.

"That the same guy's been there all along?" Bobby said.

"I doubt it."

"Hard to tell, they all look alike. Shirttails belted in hard, stick up the butt, buzzed hair. 'Look, Ma—I'm a *soul*-jur!'" Bobby's gaze shifted. "Who's the nurse with the pink hair?"

"Nursing assistant. Marcia."

"She's a sweetheart. And except for that ring that makes it look like she's got a booger hanging out of her nose all the time, damned attractive."

"I don't think you're currently on the market."

"Never have been, Doc. Never likely to have a two-car garage, a nice gas grill for the patio, or a PTA membership either." He looked up at the TV, where a bulky dark form peered from behind trees that were little more than another bulky dark form. "Second day of a horror-movie marathon. With the sound off, it's almost watchable. Loved these things when I was a kid."

His head turned to the IV bags. "Peeing like a son of a bitch, all this stuff they keep running into me."

Back my way. "Like I said—we call it landing. Always a hard one. You come in off mission, everything's been so focused, now it's all loose and unconnected, flapping in the wind. You can't get hold of it, can't make sense of how pale it all is. Because the color's gone."

I'd heard bipolars say much the same things about their manic phases.

A cluster of organ notes broke through the lowered volume, pulling our eyes back to the TV. Hikers had come across an eviscerated body. One of them caught sight of movement behind the trees, but when he looked that way, there was nothing.

"That's another thing we're trained to do well," Bobby said.

"Find bodies?"

"Bodies are never in short supply. Disappear, I meant. Here one moment, gone the next."

"But not truly gone."

"Unseen." Bobby nodded toward the window. "What's over there, behind those doors?"

"Cardiac care."

"They've been having trouble, couple or three hours now. X-ray's been here twice with their backhoe. Multiple guys and gals toting red plastic trays. Lab, I'm thinking."

"Probably so."

"Someone over there about to find out how frail our hold is."

On-screen, sheriff's men had come across a shallow cave, its floor scattered with the remains of small mammals, its rear wall half-covered with what looked to be the script of some unknown language.

"It's the beast's journal," Bobby said. "How it got to be where and what it is."

Not understanding, I shook my head.

"The writing on the wall." He gestured to the screen, reached for the urinal. "Sometimes I wish they'd left the damn catheter in. Or maybe," he said moments later, capping the urinal and returning it to the bedside table, "maybe it's just advertising. A legal disclaimer of responsibility. A recruitment poster."

He settled back, eyes on the ceiling.

"You grow up in Willnot, you hear a lot of stories about the government and its agencies. Covert activities, clandestine agendas. Surveillance. Assassination. Gets so you don't give it much thought. And eighty percent of it's bullshit, of course. But then someone gets swelled up with attitude, all indignant and shocked, and all you can do is look at them and think: You're surprised that the powerful do whatever they can to stay that way? That they justify it as somehow being for the greater good? What fucking world do you people live in?"

Bobby's eyes closed.

"Never once do you suspect that someday the world's going to flip head over ass."

On-screen, the creature stood on a hill in moonlight, listening. To traffic sounds from the interstate far away? To the howl of another like itself from deep within the woods?

"I know you're not a psychiatrist, but you had some training, right?"

"In med school, sure. Kibble. No meat."

"And you know most of these kids. Figured I'd sound you out, get your take on this."

Behind Sheriff Hobbes, the radio crackled into activity.

"It's what, nine? And you're still at the office?"

"Sue's in Minnesota visiting parents, took the dog with her. House is like walking around inside an empty oil drum."

What he'd called to tell me was that over the past week people had been finding deep, freshly dug holes. Back in the woods, on dormant farmland, behind the long-shuttered Boat-n-Bait—all around. First one he was called to see, he just shook his head. Along about the fourth he made the connection: it looked like the hole out by the gravel pit where we found the bodies. So he started random patrolling, late last night caught Seth and Cissie Reynolds in the act, hauled them home for a sitdown with parents, and learned that this was the new go-to among the town's teenagers. They'd sneak out at night, do their best to replicate the hole by the gravel pit.

What, the sheriff wanted to know, was that all about? "They can't just get tattoos like other kids? TP houses? Con someone into buying them a six-pack and have a party?"

"Did you ask them?"

"Five or six times."

"And?"

"Shrugs."

Typical adolescent fascination with death and the forbidden stepping up to the plate? But also an offbeat sense of connection to peers and, ultimately, to the community. Identification by transgression. Not sentiments that I shared with Sheriff Hobbes. Instead we talked about what could be done, counseling, school assemblies and the like, agreeing in the end that it was best to let it run its course, the kids would soon be on to something else.

John Updike wrote that while we all remain tragically alone, it's imperative to go on making signs through the glass. The kids were doing that with their diggings. None of our attempts at communication amount to a lot more.

And going on is what it's all about.

I hung up thinking about Jules Mawby the day before, and Bobby that afternoon, people who go on when it all gets to be too much. Then Ted Holmes.

Ted was Richard's partner before me. Ted had contracted HIV but was doing well with the new-generation drugs till esophageal cancer came along in its wake, early signs and symptoms initially attributed to side effects from the meds so that the cancer was well along when discovered. After months of treatment, a battery of drugs, and enough radiation that he claimed to glow in the dark at night and keep Richard awake, Ted showed up one day with a T-shirt that read I'VE HAD ENOUGH, THANK YOU, copies of which he distributed to friends. Richard still has his. He wears it whenever things go their bleakest.

15

YESTERDAY IN THE school cafeteria of a nondescript small town in Ohio, a sixteen-year-old pulled a gun from his Fender Champ lunchbox and began firing, while at a restaurant just down the street an anonymous man called the waitress over and paid the check for a family of four seated nearby, two of the children with special needs.

In Willnot, Richard and I sat over a late breakfast of biscuits (late because I had a compound fracture to attend to following an early-morn automobile accident, biscuits because I hadn't made them in weeks and decided to put an end to Richard's mawkish complaints) listening to news.

Saturday. The day stretched out ahead of us, Richard remarked, like a sun-shot mesa. This came after he urged me yet again to tell the story of my grandfather pouring blackstrap molasses over the saucer-sized biscuits served up by my grandmother every morning for sixty-plus years of his life.

"And just what have you been reading, to come up with that?" I asked. He hadn't lifted it from what was currently on his bedside table, *My Life with Pygmies*, a collection of comic essays over which he had snorted so terribly that I once took the book away from him and hid it under the clothes hamper.

"I'll footnote the source later."

"You've gone postmodern on me?"

"We must stir the pot, or the stew will stick and burn." And with a finger he sketched a backward 2 in the air. Second footnote.

But the languidly unrolling afternoon, mesa, midden, or otherwise, was not to be. There it lay in the rearview mirror. I was back at the hospital by 1 PM.

"We don't know," Clay told me, working charge that shift. "Marcia was in for vitals at eleven. He was watching TV, nothing amiss. She DC'd monitors then, per orders."

"And he DC'd himself sometime thereafter."

"Between then and lunch, which came around twelve thirty."

"He couldn't have walked out in his hospital gown without being noticed. His own clothes were ruined."

Clay nodded. "And it's not like everyone here didn't know who he was."

By this time the FBI had joined us in the person of Theodora Ogden, the fourth estate close behind as she and Joel Stern stepped from elevator and stairwell within moments of one another. Before the elevator door fully opened, Agent Ogden was asking about the officer assigned to Bobby.

"Bathroom break apparently," Clay said. "Then a set-to broke out down the hall, guy's wallet is missing, he's screaming at his roommate, blaming him. Officer Shubb interceded, calmed them both down."

Joel Stern spoke up. "A diversion."

"Of course it was. The wallet turned out to be misplaced, right?"

Clay nodded.

"And clothes will be found missing elsewhere."

Shortly thereafter we learned from Officer Shubb that Bobby had left by a service entrance wearing scrubs. He'd given a kid hanging out there $5 for his bike, told him he'd leave it at the diner on Marvel Street.

"After which," Officer Shubb said, "he's gone. Vaporizes."

No footprints. No afterimage.

Scrubs later found balled up in the trash of the bathroom at KwikStop, Cindy at the dollar store nearby recalling someone who was in doctor pajamas, yeah, bought khaki pants, a flannel shirt, $14.98 according to the ticket she fished out of the register, shoes didn't fit she remembered, he was slopping around in them.

"Bulletins are out all over," Agent Ogden said. "But these guys don't get seen unless they want to."

Joel Stern had been eavesdropping on a conversation across the room. Now he turned back. "Of all the places Sergeant Lowndes might have gone, he came back here. Not too wild a surmise to think he *did* want to be seen."

Something moved in the darkness, something I almost but not quite caught sight of. Something I could hear breathing. There at the edge of consciousness for a time, then inescapable. Stentorious *came to mind. As the sounds of breathing grew ever louder.*

As the breathing became Richard's beside me.

I got up to pee. Prostate showing signs of wear and tear. Time to check my PSA. Dickens had come with, and followed me into the kitchen. Planes and edges in the backyard grabbed at slivers of the full moon's light.

Other people have dreams that they're naked in the class-room, lost on almost-familiar streets, fleeing the unseen. I hadn't been fleeing the unseen, I'd been peering into dark corners and recesses looking for it. Rooting about in cupboards, closets, and clothes hampers. Then in the dream was at some conference among attendees with unkempt hair, impeccable credentials and terrifying sincerity, sitting on a folding chair on an expanse of darkly floral carpet chewed by thousands of such chair legs.

"It all depends," a moderator says, and I realize the moderator is Richard, "on whether you believe that governments form to protect individuals from implicit violence, establishing order by forcibly restraining those impulses, or that governments in fact centralize and monopolize violence to themselves. Does the nation exist to serve its citizens, or to regulate, to proscribe? In a word, is the state's primary purpose to allow—or to prevent?"

From the stage he points to me for response. All heads turn.

"Can't sleep?"

It took me a moment to realize it wasn't the dream, wasn't my memory of the dream, any longer. *Now* had bled back in. Richard stood in the doorway, one eye half-closed, the other squinting.

"I was having a dream misdelivered from some social scien-tist's head."

"The horror! At least you had Dickens to keep you company. What time is it, anyway?"

"Sixish, I'm guessing. Light outside's just starting to change."

"So I have to be up in an hour anyway. Whatever could we do with that hour?"

Life is filled with choice and challenge.

16

MONDAY WAS BLOWOUT day. Hernias, bleeding varicose veins, Charlene Spencer's "beauty mole" that popped and started oozing something that looked for all the world like guacamole.

"Not good?" Charlene said.

"Questionable. Green's great in the wild, not so much in bodies."

By 1:40 we'd cleared the office and Maryanne went down the street to Frisky's, just under the wire since Mabel closed down at two so she could catch her TV shows, to bring back lunch. Five bites in, moments after Maryanne and I had opened the accounts-payable file to go over it as we ate, the phone rang. Maryanne answered, listened, then said "Principal Chorley wants to know where you are."

"Obviously he knows where I am."

"You're supposed to judge the science fair."

"Did I say I'd do that?"

"*Someone* said you would."

And I had a pretty good idea who that someone, who'd forgotten to tell or remind me, was.

"I'm really not much of a science guy, you know."

"Lamar . . . You're a doctor."

"Different game. Different gloves."

"Okay, then you're the closest thing we have." Shaking her head, mock amusement floating above like a cartoon caption, she said to the phone "He'll be right there" and to me "They're waiting."

Blowups were big at the science fair too. Two model active volcanoes (though one more closely resembled a lava lamp), a self-invented, all-natural bug bomb and, in true patchwork Willnot-libertarian-leftist form, the four-step diorama of a nuclear power plant disaster. First prize went to the last, which deserved it on the basis of effort and invested hours alone, never mind imaginative content. Exacting as the scale was, you could make out terrified features on the tiny faces of those fleeing the plant and, in the final representation, set ten years later, evidence of physical deformity and disease.

The entry's creator, Bo Johnsson, who went by BJ, was a model himself, the guy we all secretly hated in high school, good at everything: first-chair clarinet, quarterback on the football team and star player on the basketball team, straight-A student, beloved by teachers, the very stuff of "why can't you be more like" heart-to-hearts. By way of snarkily thanking him for volunteering me, I brought that up with Richard and he said Yeah, he knew that guy, briefly he'd been that guy.

"Football? You?"

"My chameleon days, sweetheart. Still doing my best back then to fit in."

"Ah, youth."

"I got over it."

"Which?"

"Both."

Well past six as we sat there, dark and light playing tag you're it across the floor, thoughts of dinner beginning to find purchase toward the fore of our minds. Earlier, Richard had brought out a bottle of Oregon-born pinot noir and poured two glasses. He'd spent late afternoon at the dentist's having a crown replaced, paying, he claimed, for Doctor Crawford's next vacation. Came home with one side of his face twice as long as the other.

Cautiously he fit glass to lips.

"Better now?" I asked.

"Not likely to trip over it as I walk, anyway."

I was lifting my glass when the phone rang.

"What do you think," Richard said. "Home security?"

"Carpet cleaning, possibly."

"Charity."

"Or a nice, juicy public opinion poll."

But it was only ER wanting to know could I possibly come in. Everyone else seemed to be busy, out of pocket, or out of sorts.

"Back soon," I told Richard.

"I'll wait dinner."

"I could stop and get us carryout."

"Whatever your heart desires. Except the wine. The rest of the wine is mine."

A man in his thirties lay handcuffed to one of the gurneys. Everything about him, his haircut, his bearing even when recumbent, screamed military. Dark, expressionless eyes followed me from doorway to bedside.

Sheriff Hobbes sat beside him. It's all gurneys and stainless-steel stools in there. The sheriff had spun the stool's seat up as far as it would go.

"You both look like the other guy."

He glanced at me, then his attention went back to the hand-cuffed man. "Say what?"

"Hard to tell which of you's the patient."

The sheriff had a gash at least two inches long on his fore-head, blood coming off, I hoped not from, one ear. The way he was clenched in on himself, he had to be in considerable pain.

Sally Bounds came out from the nurses' station to join us. "They both are. But Roy, bullheaded as ever, won't let us touch him."

"Explain to him that in here we're the law?"

"Repeatedly."

I nodded to the man on the gurney. "You splinted the arm?"

Sally shook her head. "Roy, before he brought him in."

"Okay. I'm going to assume, Sheriff, that this isn't a case of your playing Good Samaritan."

"Handcuffs give it away?"

"That and the tussle. You have to be sporting one hell of a headache. Any dizziness?"

"I'll be fine, Lamar. It's this man you need to see to."

As I set about doing so, the sheriff told me what happened. The man on the gurney never flinched, never reacted, eyes moving steadily back and forth from my hands to my face. *Watching* would be a poor descriptor. *Observing.*

He'd got a call, the sheriff said, from Audrey at the MaxiMart. Fellow was in there to pay for gas, picked up some PowerBars and water, and as he came up the aisle, another man turned the corner, tripped, and almost ran into him. It was there just a second, Audrey said. In his eyes. In the way his body pulled into itself. Audrey knew that look, he'd seen it too often before to miss or mistake it.

102

Now, Audrey's not quite right, you know that as well as I do, the sheriff said. And you know why.

Sun and sand, I said.

So, Audrey never having called me like that before, I figure I'll go have a talk with this fellow, see how he liked his PowerBars, see is there anything I can do for him. If he's still around.

He isn't, not at first, but then as I'm swinging back by the hospital there's the pearl-colored Honda Audrey told me about, pulling out of the parking lot. I follow him to the old Wayfare Motel, the Starlight or whatever they're calling it now, he enters room eight, I go and knock on the door. When it opens I see he's got a duffel bag laid out on the bed, about packed up to go, looks like. I don't say anything, we just stand there. Then suddenly an arm's coming toward me. I sidestep, then walk back into the arm with my whole weight behind, slam it into the door-frame. The arm's broken, but it doesn't slow him down. I got lucky. I also got the baton from the trunk that I'd stuck in the back of my belt.

Which explains, I said, these contusions on the back of his skull.

It was kind of like hitting on a rock, Lamar. Took some doing. While I'm waiting for Andrew and his ambulance I sniff out the car. Under the mat in the trunk, in the tire well, there's a broken-down rifle. Small caliber. Thing's like a shark. Designed for one thing and one thing only.

"Did he talk?" I asked when the sheriff finished.

"Hasn't said a word."

"This arm has to be reduced and set, which means a trip to OR. And a marathon trip to radiology first. The arm, of course. Skull series. Pretty much everything, just to be safe."

"I'll go along," the sheriff said.

"In a manner of speaking, yes, you will. Same workup for you."

"I can't—"

"Shut up, Roy. Or I'll switch the handcuffs over to you."

Sally came out from the station smiling. "On their way," she said.

17

I HEARD WHEN his breathing changed and knew he was awake. Nothing showed on the monitors.

"That sheriff of yours is thirty pounds of hard-ass in a five-pound sack."

"Things are tough out here on the frontier."

"Like they're not elsewhere?"

I remembered the way his eyes had observed me back in ER— as they swept over my face, checked for exits, fastened for a moment on activities past the room's window. Somewhere across the way, the monotonous, soft clang of monitor alarms sounded. No code or stat called overhead, though, no scurry of movement in that direction.

I watched him look down along his body. Move his fingers.

"We pinned the arm," I said. "You won't have any loss of mobility, should be back on full charge in six weeks or less. Moderate hematomas. Mild concussion. Sheriff's good too, already back on the street."

"Half an hour more, neither of us would ever have been off them."

"Life rarely gets the detour signs up in time."

"Everywhere I've been, all I've done, I come here to this sneeze of a town and get taken down by an old man." He lifted his other arm the six inches or so the cuffs allowed, demonstrating. "Meanwhile, don't you have lives to save? People to sew back together?"

"Slow day."

We listened to phones ring, watched the tanklike progress of a portable X-ray machine nosing its way through carts, chairs, an emergency ventilator, trash cans, and scales toward a far room. The tech kept peeking out from behind. She'd lug to the right and hit something, look to see, correct to the left and hit something else.

"When he was shot, Bobby told me it was an old friend's way of saying hello."

"So Bobby's okay."

"You know he is. Okay and out of sight."

"All the devil dogs on his trail? Behind the lines, in country, you keep moving."

"He had friends here."

"Friends are fence posts. Hold you in place, make you visible. And the ones he has elsewhere are Kong-size."

I'd heard *Cong*, like *Viet Cong*, but before I said anything, he added: "As in King."

Dogs. Giant gorillas. "And what's Billygoat?"

He shifted on the bed, trying for a sweet spot that wasn't there. "Came up one of those days you're sitting in your own sweat and stink drinking beer, BS-ing, waiting for something to happen. Kings of the hill, someone said, that's us. Even if the hill's like a foot high, someone else said. But we gotta get up there and keep the others off. Because that's what billy goats do."

I walked out assuming I wouldn't see him again, so I wasn't surprised when the call came. The guard had stepped off for a moment to refill his coffee thermos, returned to an empty room. Our patient slipped the handcuffs, deactivated monitors, evaporated. *You keep moving.*

"Man's got a broken arm, damaged parts, no resources, how far's he gonna get?" the officer said. State trooper Stanton, standing in for the sheriff, rationalizing.

"I suspect he's gone much farther with far worse."

We all have our own way of dealing with what troubles us. Sadness, frustration, despair, anger. Richard's way of dealing with just about everything is humor. That night when I told him about the second disappearance, his comment was that someone, or some thing, was collecting snipers, more or less quoting Charles Fort, a favorite among the science fiction clan back in the day. One measures a circle beginning anywhere, rains of frogs, mysterious disappearances. Nothing in religion, science, or philosophy that was more than the proper thing to wear for a while; the Earth is a farm and we're someone else's property. The great-grandfather of crankdom.

We talked more about Bobby and what the second sniper had said, and I told Richard about the epigraph to one of my father's books: "Everyone we meet is fighting a battle about which we know nothing." The quotation wasn't attributed, and when years later I tried to look it up, I found near misses going back to at least 1903.

In that novel, *Good Fortune*, a man has the gift of seeing the future. This began as flashes when he was a child, we're told, before he had words, before he could know or say what the visions were, and steadily grew. The book opens with him standing at the edge of a clearing beneath a bright moon, desultorily addressing gods he doesn't believe in, beseeching them to take the gift from him, allow him to live without these winds blowing in constantly from the future, crowding out his days and years. His life.

Back then my father's habit was to count out two hundred first sheets, two hundred seconds for carbons and, when the stacks got down to the last ten, to start winding things up, so one hundred and ninety-nine pages later, for the first time, we see the gun. It glints in the moonlight as the protagonist lifts it. It's as though he is waiting for something, and soon, behind, he hears the scuffle of his wife's feet on loose gravel.

"Don't," she says.

They stand silently. Traffic sounds come from far away, as though from another, reasonable, purposeful world.

"I won't," he says, and the book concludes. We never know if his inaction results from making the choice, or if it's simply because he knows in advance how his life *will* end.

That book was a favorite of my father's friend Jan Wilford who used to come visit us periodically in Elaine, in Willnot, in Marvel or Walnut Corner. Jan was, my father said, the best person alive at destroying the world. He'd done it with garbage, with a rogue asteroid, with sentient clouds, black ice, tiny mutant crickets, even grass. Once, uncharacteristically, my father apologized for not having read Jan's latest novel. "Why would you?" he said. "It's just like all the others." And sitting there with beers, moon a flat white disk balanced atop the trees, an owl commenting from one nearby, they laughed.

As did Richard and I.

"You've truly had an interesting life, my love," he said. "Keep pulling out these stories. Your father going to see the editor of *Galaxy* in his apartment because he hadn't left it in ten years, or pacing that writer in his car on the way somewhere together because the guy—what was his name?—couldn't ride in a machine on a holy day."

"Avram Davidson."

"Right."

"They were quackingly odd ducks."

"You ever hear from any of them?"

"No reason I would. Most are dead now."

"I feel as though I know some of them, from the stories."

"They were like all the rest of us, many different people jammed into a single container. You see the one looking out at you at the time."

"True enough." Dickens wandered in to see what we were doing and, unimpressed, collapsed on the floor inside the door. "You ever consider why your mother's never in those stories?"

I realized that Richard was gazing over my shoulder, off into the distance. "It would seem you have a gentleman caller."

I turned to look, out across the yard to the garage.

Bobby.

Where he'd stood the night of the party. Where I'd seen him only because and only when he'd wanted me to.

He saw I was watching, nodded once, and was gone.

18

IF SOMEONE WAS collecting snipers as Richard by way of Charles Fort suggested, then someone else was shipping in neurotics and worriers as replacements. Streams of them poured through my office on their way to the sea, to the extent that when one with what seemed a real medical issue showed up late in the day (acute diverticulitis, to every appearance), I all but pounced. We'd passed her along for lab work, X-rays and a return engagement the next morning, and Maryanne was about to drop the CLOSED sign when a van pulled up at curbside just outside. A refugee from the previous decade, off-white with logo and lettering from prior commercial use showing ghostlike beneath.

I shrugged when Maryanne looked at me. Why not? She unlocked the door. A scouting party dismounted from the van. A couple in their fifties, an older gentleman bent bowlike, as though by a string running from forehead to feet.

Explaining that we were about to close up shop, we seated them and asked how we could help.

The couple looked at one another, then at the older man, then back at me. Blink, blink, blink.

"He stinks," the woman said.

The man's father, Merritt, resided in an assisted-care center in nearby Greer. He'd been there almost a year, no complaints, for what it was the place was okay. On a visit last month they began to notice something. That he smelled different.

"He stank," the woman said.

"Body chemistry changes with age. Diet can make a huge difference. Not to mention medications."

"We asked about that," she said. "The meds, I mean. He's getting what he's been on for years. Beta-blocker, daily aspirin, insulin."

I looked at Merritt. His skin reminded me of old guitar tops, color altered by time, lighter some places, darkened others, lacquerlike surface cracks running every which way.

"Don't give half a damn what the date is or who the president is," he said.

"Okay."

"Just saying, before you ask. Thing's simple, really, no big mystery to it: Old pipes stink. I should know."

"Merritt was a plumber."

The old man didn't actually snort, but his expression strongly suggested it. "When I had a life."

"You think that place comes cheap—"

"That's enough, Mildred." It was the first time the younger man, Merritt's son, had spoken. Ceremoniously his wife began investigating the condition of ceilings, paint, and fixtures. "Why don't we wait out here while you have a look at Dad, Doctor Hale?"

Back in the exam room, Merritt turtled into the chair across from my desk, head and neck jutting forward, thin legs adangle.

"What, no take-off-your-clothes? No cold-steel exploratory devices? Are you really a doctor?"

"Are you a stinkbug?"

His mouth didn't laugh, but his eyes did.

"How are things going at the care center?"

"Fun place. Full of good cheer, sunny tomorrows."

I waited.

"When I was a kid," he said, "I couldn't wait to get to school. Ten minutes after I came through the front door, I'd be packed and ready to go back. Everybody thought I must have gears missing. But school was flat-out a joy compared to what I had at home. Same with the care center. It works."

"So why are you here?"

He made to sit up straighter in the chair. I saw no improvement and he registered none. But a man's gotta keep trying.

"Mildred's a sweet girl, good to my son. And she means well. But change, change for her is scary. Sneaks up from behind, never what it seems, makes a fool of you."

"And change makes you smelly?"

"Comes back to a woman—like so many things in life. Nellie, my wife, she died over twenty years ago, and there hasn't been anyone since. Not till now."

"At the center."

"Yep. Like me, she gets around just fine. Lot of 'em don't. Broke her hip, but then worked her butt off to get back. You'd see her all times of the day scooting her walker down to the PT room. Worked in a health-food store till she was fifty-six and got pushed aside to make way for Amber. Amber looked about twelve years old and had green hair."

Now it made sense. A health-food store. "You're taking supplements."

He nodded. "Protein tablets, zinc and minerals, a whole alphabet of vitamins, pills of this and that flower or weed or grass.

Handfuls of the things four, five times a day. When I started taking them, she said before long I'd smell like she did."

"And you haven't shared this with your family?"

"None of their business. Don't see me asking what goes on in *their* room at night."

We talked a bit longer, then went out to rejoin the family, to whom I said that, save for the arthritis, Merritt was in good health. Diabetes under control, everything working as it should. I did suggest that, as he'd been on the atenolol for some time, he be sure to ask to have new blood work done.

The daughter-in-law opened her mouth but shut it at a glance from her husband, who soundly thanked me. I walked them to the door and asked how they'd found their way to me. One of the nurses that took care of Merritt made the recommendation, the son said. "Said you weren't like most doctors."

I told Richard about that when he called minutes later.

"Wow. *Not like most doctors.* You should put that on your Facebook page. If you had a Facebook page."

"What's up?"

"Athletics rally. I ditched and got home early. You want I should cook?"

"Seized by a restless urge, are we?"

"More like a notion. A passing fancy."

"Or we could go out."

"A peculiar whim . . ."

"We do, of course, have three days of leftovers."

"Ah, yes, the world-famous Hale Diet. Leftovers every meal, where *do* they all come from? Point made. I'll go in the kitchen, see what falls off the shelves."

"Is that Dickens I hear?"

"Sounds just like him, doesn't it? His understudy. A

mockingbird who has practiced long and hard and now is ready for his time center stage. He was on the front porch when I got home. Dickens may be in love."

"He hears himself in the mirror?"

"Or maybe he just wants a snack."

Days lumbered on, as they will. Miracles happened in the corners of lives, longings slumbered in our hearts. Wednesday night Richard announced that he'd had enough of politicians pissing one another's doorsteps and CEOs getting retirement packages of millions while workers couldn't feed their kids or afford health care, and it was time for an embargo on news. Critically so. He was beginning to despise humankind.

Dinner had been a fanciful omelet of andouille, shaved Parmesan and pears, that and a cucumber-tomato salad. More concocted than cooked, he insisted. "Cooking implies some level or pretension of artistry. What you see before you was not created, it was built. Assembled. As from a kit."

Thursday he was suspended for insubordination when, at a staff meeting, he could not refrain from addressing the principal's fifth or sixth vapid statement, and on Monday was reinstated, the principal that morning having been terminated for "undisclosed reasons." The school board asked if Richard might be willing to serve as acting principal.

"I'm a teacher, not an administrator," he said. "They want to take me away from what I do well, put me at a desk doing something I suck at?"

That no one else cared anywhere near as much about the school or the kids as he did, went without saying. It sounded to me as though they expected him to do both jobs. That went unsaid too.

115

Periodically over the next few days I spotted Agent Ogden moving about town, stepping onto a porch, sitting fence-post-straight behind the wheel of her rented Hyundai, but we had no further contact. On Monday, about the same time that Richard was meeting with the school board, Joel Stern showed up at the office to let me know he was shipping out.

"The American dream's moved on again," he said. "Back the way we came, to the great Midwest."

"And you're in hot pursuit."

"Tepid." He had elected not to sit, stood poking at a model on the shelf, one of the expensive show-and-tells that drug companies and manufacturers used to hand out by the boxful, a sickly pink foot and ankle with about four inches of leg bones. When you pushed at it, the ankle went out of joint, then moments later popped back in.

"What's going on in the heartland?"

"Corn. The fifties good life. With an occasional school shooting or tasty mass murder." He moved from the foot model to framed diplomas on the wall by the shelves. "And some really good people."

"Good people are everywhere."

"You'd be shocked how long it took for me to learn that." He came up to the desk and held out his hand. "I wanted to say a proper good-bye, Doctor Hale. And to ask . . . Early next year a small press up in Seattle is bringing out a collection of my essays. I'd like to send you one, if that's all right with you."

"I'll look forward to it."

"Then you're number one on the list." He smiled. "It's a short, short list. Please tell your friend I wish him the best of luck."

"Bobby?"

"I meant Richard, but yes, the sergeant too."

"You know about Richard's work situation?"

"A large part of what I do consists of hanging around, listening, looking sideways. Much of the rest, the formal interviews, checking public records, all that, it's three-quarters misdirection. Stirring the pot. Shaking the tree."

As I watched him go, out of the office and along the street where he stopped to chat for a moment with Old Ezra, it came to me that, without having previously given it much thought, I liked Joel Stern. A man not easily deceived or distracted—not by growls, not by slogans or sound bites, not by white noise. Not even by the scripts running continously in his head, by his own preconceptions.

19

GRAFFITI SPRAY-PAINTED ON the wall read JESUS SAVES. Someone had come along, slashed through the first S in SAVES and drawn in an oversize R above.

"Never underestimate the power of an editor," Richard said. "Is Jesus the subject, or an adjective?"

Having blockaded news, we sought enlightenment wherever it might be found.

I was dropping Richard off to pick up his car following carburetor work and new brake pads. Which was also revision, as he pointed out. Standing to the left of the garage, the wall with the graffiti had separated it from a drive-through of some sort. That was mostly gone now: a cement foundation, jagged bits of walls, half a roundabout of driveway.

"Thanks for the ride," Richard said as we pulled in, one hand on the strap of his backpack, other on the door handle.

"Whatever happened to my Creature photograph?" I asked.

I'd had it from childhood, a photo probably shot as a gag on the set, showing the Creature from the Black Lagoon and the female lead passionately embracing. The Creature had her in its arms, dipping her back; she was in a swoon, leg kicked up and back, as they kissed.

"I believe I may have put it safely away. As I did with that horrid blue dress shirt of yours."

"Jealous?"

"Do you hear the silence streaming from me?"

"And of which, the Creature or her?"

"Irrelevant, considering that I'm better looking than both. Well, her at least. Lizard guy *was* kind of a hunk, now that I think of it."

An overhead door ran almost the whole of the garage's front. With a steady low grind it ascended. The operator secured the pulley chain and waved Richard in.

"Where did you get it, anyway?" Richard said.

"The photo? It was a gift from my mother."

"Ah, yes. Your mother."

"She just thought I should have it, she said."

"You never told me that."

"It didn't occur to me till a lot later that it might be a coded message."

Richard wound the backpack strap in his hand and climbed out. "Isn't everything?"

It certainly seemed so that day. A patient I'd seen a couple of times before for wide-ranging complaints sitting across the desk from me wondering (as he looked toward the window) if it all might not be in his head, in the office today because (glancing down at the floor) he couldn't seem to care about anything anymore. A refund check in the mail from a bill I'd neither received nor paid. Writing a script only to learn that I'd used the last page of the last prescription pad; we'd neglected to reorder. Four rings with hang-ups, Maryanne told me, in just over an hour.

Codes?

Indecipherable signals?

Or happenstance—like most of life.

And then there was the the final report from Sebastian Daiche's team that the sheriff brought over, asking for my help in translating it. A slurry of medical terminology mixed with legal phrases that effectively swallowed their own tails, the first Latinate, the second mandarin, determining somewhere among them that:

There were three to four bodies, all Caucasian, all young-adult males.

All went into the ground at approximately the same time.

Cause of death could not be ascribed.

No identification was possible.

The sheriff and I were standing by the window. An unfamiliar recent-model Ford pickup eased by in the street, two rifles in the rack behind the driver, one passenger. Roy tracked it until it passed out of sight with a turn onto Poplar. I handed the report back to him.

"We've reached the end of our knowledge then," I said. "It's over. What about the kids, any of them still out there digging?"

"Not so's I've seen or heard."

"Moving along."

"The kids are, anyway. Others, not so much. There's been talk about putting up some kind of memorial."

"A memorial. We don't even know who the bodies were. Or why."

"That's part of the idea, I think."

"*Whose* idea? Where did this come from?"

"Beats me. But it's around."

Richard told me later that day that the kids at school were

talking about the memorial too, the rumor being that a contest was going to be held for its design.

Just after five I was on rounds at the hospital, playing dodge-it with food carts from hallway to hallway, glimpsing on TV after TV multiple versions of essentially the same news. As I passed a waiting room, Sunil signaled me to hold on, excused himself from the family he'd been sitting with, and moments later joined me. Sunil's the closest thing we have to a house chaplain. He wore a mahogany-colored corduroy suit the like of which I'd not seen in twenty years. I'd long suspected that Sunil was on first-name terms with a watchful thrift-shop employee.

"Their daughter," he said. "Last night she got out of bed and started walking into walls. They heard the thuds, found her in her room. She'd back up four or five steps and walk into the wall again. When they tried to talk to her, all they got was what sounded like strings of vowels. Not much that can be done for her here."

"She needs neurology."

"Exactly. They're getting her ready for a transfer to University. Wanted to ask you, who should she see up there?"

"Who saw her here?"

"Dr. Bullard."

"Dan will refer to the same person I would, Kate Cross. No one better, anywhere. I'll give her a call."

"Thanks, Lamar. But . . ."

I'd started away, turned back. Made room for a lab tech and candy striper to pass.

"That wasn't all I wanted to see you about. A visitor turned up at the church yesterday, late afternoon, no one else around. I came upon him sitting in the rear pew. Texting, or reading. On what they call a tablet these days, I think. Asked if it was okay for him to be there. We talked, and your name came up."

122

"Did his?"

"Bobby."

"Bobby never struck me as the kind to hang out in churches. Wasn't much given to religion."

"I don't think that's what he was seeking there. Or what he was bringing." Which was about as mystical as Sunil's pronouncements ever got. "He said if I saw you, to be sure and tell you hello for him."

"Which you took literally enough to seek me out."

"I had the feeling it wasn't figurative, Lamar. Nor simple sentiment."

So: Code again?

And Bobby was still around. Why? I walked off wondering.

A while later, I was leaving Radiology after checking pictures of ten-year-old Dominic's dislocated hip when Vinny approached me. A small wonder, since he rarely left his office.

Joint problems in a young person are particularly worrisome, prompting all manner of speculation about skeletal defects, congenital conditions, the possibility of RA, spondylitis, or one of their ugly cousins.

"I heard you were in house," Vinny said, "wanted you to see this." *This* being a letter on Forward Foundation stationery.

Dear Mr. Parelli:

It has been my intention for some time now to write and thank you for the excellent, concerned care I was fortunate enough to receive at Bielecki Hospital. I cannot overstate this— the care, or my appreciation—in light of the fact that your concerted actions saved my life.

Following recovery and intensive physical therapy, I am back near 100% now, soon to ship out again with the crew to an excavation site in Turkey, where we will be investigating tales of an entire village population killed and buried in a single grave. I'm very much looking forward to getting back on the horse.

Once again, please accept my profound thanks, and please pass thanks along to Dr. Hale and, in turn, to your entire staff.

Sidney M. Patmore

P.S. Seb Daiche has asked that I convey to Dr. Hale his apologies that we were unable to be of more help with the bodies there in Willnot.

Richard and I arrived home within minutes of one another, poured a couple of glasses of pinot noir, and headed out to the patio, where he told me the car was running smooth as glass, he was as of today acting principal, and his predecessor had threatened the school board with litigation. In turn I told him about Sunil, the report on the bodies, and Mr. Patmore's letter. Darkness nudged at every edge. We sat watching the flash of diaphanous wings against light bleeding from the house behind us. Presently I went in to pee, Richard to refill glasses. Coming round from the kitchen, he stood in the bathroom doorway.

"Two-fisted?" I said.

"Always carry a spare. Buddy system. Plan ahead for possible spills." He gestured in slow motion, so as to minimize sloshing, with the left-hand glass. "If you need help putting that away . . ."

"Not at the moment."

I finished and we went back outside, where Dickens looked on intently, pondering whether chasing moths was worth the multiple efforts required. A bat shot into sight like a thrown grenade, scooping up insects at light's margin, just as suddenly gone.

20

AS THOUGH MAGICALLY summoned by my mention of it, neurology moved in to supplant sniper collecting and coded signals as patients presented with:

A painful, progressive ringing in the ears and—patently— balance problems, strongly suggesting Ménière's disease;

Blurred and double vision, muscle spasms and general fatigue, symptoms so nonspecific that they might be anything, or nothing, but that in the context felt to me like MS;

Tremors and a gait that, given their nature and the patient's age, given also the constant circular motion of index finger and thumb called pill-rolling, almost certainly indicated Parkinson's.

All these oddly enough in two days, before we fell back to the accustomed run of virus, rash and sniffles, angina, blood where blood shouldn't be, UTIs, asthma, menopause, prolapses, loss of feeling, swellings, and pain. Performed an emergency appy in there somewhere, set an arm, and sent a three-year-old with wandering eye to vision therapists at University Hospital.

Meanwhile the days proceeded much like a master pratfaller tripping over hassocks, chairs, and folds in the carpet on his way across the room only to recover, again and again, in the last moment. Groups of every sort, religious, regional, political, fraternal, went on beating at the tribal drum, rallying to themselves all those who believed, felt, and dressed like them. And all of us went on seeking some form or fashion of Camus's invincible summer.

Wearing his new hat as official Bossman and to the chorus of "When am I supposed to find time to teach," Richard's daily stories now were not of students and course work but of tempests brewed painstakingly in teacups, eggshell egos, counselings, and intercessions, so when on a Wednesday I arrived home to find him doing a fair take on Wednesday's child filled with woe, I assumed it to be more of the same.

But Nathan, the ant-mill kid and twelve-year-old freethinker, had gone missing.

Nathan ran the household when their mother was at work. Fixed breakfast, saw sister Chloe off to school properly and on time. But that morning, Chloe roused when her radio alarm went off and found a note on the kitchen table saying he had to get away to think about things and her breakfast was over by the stove. Chloe ate—toast and a plain omelet swaddled in aluminum foil—and was almost done with the Cheerios she'd got for herself when she thought she might ought to call her mother at the diner. Mom called the school. Acting principal Richard caught the call.

So everyone, Richard said, is looking for Nathan.

At which point—we were sitting in the kitchen—I glanced up and saw a young man passing by the window as he stepped onto the porch. I went to the door and opened it before he could knock.

"Nathan," Richard said.

Bobby stood beyond, in the yard. "This is where he asked to come."

Richard gave the boy a quick hug and, realizing who Bobby was, introduced himself, shaking hands, as they came in. Nathan sat at the table. Bobby remained standing against the wall at (I couldn't help but notice) an angle well out of line of sight from the windows.

I got bottles of water from the fridge for both of them. "Not every day that two missing persons show up together on our porch."

"You're okay?" Richard asked.

Nathan nodded, emptied his bottle in two gulps.

"We need to call your mother." Richard went into the living room for his phone, came back and motioned Nathan to follow him.

"I got your message," I said.

"From the pastor."

I gestured toward the front room, toward Nathan. "He *is* okay, right?"

"Fine. Confused."

"About?"

"Come on, Doc. He's smart. Sees what goes on around him, how it doesn't fit what he's told." Bobby looked out into the yard. "Hope you don't mind my bringing him here."

"We appreciate it. Richard was worried."

"And hope my having been here doesn't bring anything else down on you."

Richard stuck his head in the door to tell me he was going to run Nathan home.

"I've been staying out in the woods," Bobby said. "Living off the land for the most part."

"With your tablet."

"Your pastor friend let me recharge." Saw in his grin a flash of the Brandon I'd known as a boy. "I don't know how much you may have figured out about what's going on."

"Not much. That the FBI's not alone in looking for you. When you got shot you said it was an old friend saying hello."

"I could count on my thumbs the number of times Carlos ever missed what he set his sights on. His handlers know it too, but what's to prove? And getting taken down by local law—which is every bit as unlikely as Carlos missing the shot—then having to skip out, that takes him out of the picture."

Bobby finished his water, held up the bottle. "You have recycle now, right?"

"In the pantry, green bin."

"Both of us," Bobby said, coming back, "declined to do what we were told. Carlos was smarter about it. Anyhow . . ." He stood where he'd been before. Not a half inch difference. "I came across the kid out there, couple of miles from anything, in a clearing that looked like it was a favorite spot for someone a long time back. Remains of a picnic table gone gray and spongy from exposure, rocks that made a kind of cook pit, part of a Styrofoam cooler with onions growing out of it.

"He looks up when he hears me, asks 'Is it okay for me to be here?' Okay by me, I tell him, and it's public land, but maybe there are parents, teachers, who are worried about him?"

"What was he doing out there?"

"Sitting. Checking out his shoes. Listening to the wind. My old friend Dell would say he was trying to feel himself a part of the world again, instead of apart from it. I think he was just trying to get the noise out of his head.

"We had a long talk. You don't meet up with many kids—hell, with many people, period—that want to talk about anything real. Most of it's dead air and white noise, he kept saying."

I waited. Listening to the wind myself, I guess.

"What got said's between the two of us, Doc, ought to stay that way. Two guys sitting together out in the woods away from it all, both carrying stuff you'd think with the gap in age, where we've been, couldn't possibly be more different, but you look close and it turns out not to be very different at all."

Bobby's head shifted suddenly as he peered out into the yard. He was silent a moment, then turned back.

"Not that I think there's much need to say what we talked about. Never took you to be in the amen corner for the great myth of progress."

"True. But I'm surprised—"

"That I'm still around? Me no less than you. Not sure why I came, or why I didn't leave the way I started to. Used to be so sure about things. You know, Doc . . ."

Traffic sounds on the street outside, a truck or heavy SUV. Bobby listened as it passed.

"You always think it's going to be some huge moral decision."

"The twenty-minute slam." When he shook his head, I went on, "Someone my father knew said that's how he wrote a hundred TV shows. Whatever the character believes, by twenty minutes into the show it folds up on him. Everything he knew was wrong. And because of that, in the last five minutes his life is changed forever. Not like that, huh?"

"Except for the change part. I knew what I was doing, the weight of it. All I wanted was to stop." Bobby straightened. "I'd better get along."

On the porch he turned back to say, "I hope your boy works it out," then stepped off into the yard and within seconds was part of the night.

21

My dear Lamar,

It's been a long time, I know, and I'm sorry. Not that I haven't been thinking about you—ever. So much conspires to pull us away from what's most important.

Could it really be that a year has passed since I told you I was moving to Kentucky? Back to Joe's cockeyed, weird and weirdly beautiful South. We've bought a house far outside town (the town itself is full to capacity at just over 500 souls) where, sitting outside in morning or late afternoon, it's not difficult to imagine that we're alone, safely tucked away from all of civilization's gears ceaselessly grinding us down. And from memory's doing the same.

Fiona fares well. No question that she misses Eldon, thinks of him constantly, but it's been months since I heard her weeping at night in her room. Robbie has recovered perhaps as much as he shall. He's 12 now—again, hard to believe. Therapists taught us, before we moved, everything we needed to know to continue his daily regimen. He walks unaided, can see to his own needs as far as hygiene, eating, dressing and such. He does fine as long as language connects to what he can touch or see, or almost: objects, routines, time of day. Whenever talk or events list toward the abstract he simply stands there. Not looking confused, or any different at all, really. Time out, more or less. Waiting for the world to get back on track, knowing that in time it will.

No day goes by but that I think how impossible was Fiona's choice in ending the pregnancy, her and Eldon's child inside her on the one hand, Robbie's extravagant needs on the other. None of us can ever know how that feels.

Well, you could.

The people here before us, longtime renters, had fig trees. We'll let them go to ruin, no doubt, but they serve to remind me of those you liked so much when you were small. What—six or seven? Back in Arkansas. You'd sit in them for hours. It was like being inside a rib cage, you said.

Is there ever a line between regret and memory, Lamar? How do we find it?

Robbie has Richard's love for animals. Each afternoon at five he goes to the kitchen, gets down the bin of dog food, and puts out three bowls of it, one red, one blue, one green. A raccoon is waiting and steps up immediately, evidencing no shyness whatsoever. The last time it came there were babies following it. Other regulars include a badger Robbie calls Adger (he can't form the b sound), a tiny yellow female cat missing most of one paw (Little One), and (as yet unnamed) a remarkably mellow skunk that tolerates and is tolerated by both Adger and Little One.

I do still hear from some of the old crowd. They ask about you. A lot of them are going or gone, of course. Do you remember Irv Palander? He wrote that series where the stove and clocks

132

and other household appliances are always talking to whatever the guy's name was—correcting him when he sets the temperature wrong, doesn't flush the toilet or wash his hands, drinks too much or stays up late. He calls every now and again. The phone will ring, it's quiet for a moment or two, then he'll say "Another one's down, Clara." And it's Henry up in Minneapolis, or Carol in Connecticut, or Kentucky Kim. No more adventures on the ice planet, their bows and arrows and energy guns are put to rest, the dystopia's shut down, their ships never again to kick-start.

I guess what they say is true, at some point when you look in the mirror you see the past. I'm sitting here thinking how many years I scolded you, when you went off to college, when you were interning at Beth Israel and doing your residency, for not writing. And now it's me who doesn't write. A year! I will try to do better, I promise.

Meanwhile, if you'd ever consider coming for a visit to this wonderfully godforsaken place, there's a spare room—even if we might have to send pictures so that we'd recognize one another. I might even, given the occasion, be driven to cook.

Love you, Lamar. Hugs for Richard.

Mom

22

TIME TO BE a responsible citizen.

Or to claim exemption.

Jury duty.

I could of course, probably without challenge, plead that my presence and ministrations were essential to the community, but that would feel a cheat. And there are other physicians to handle whatever comes along.

So I found myself Monday at 9 AM sitting behind glass in a waiting room on the second story of the courthouse two towns over with *National Treasure* playing on the large screen at one side of the room and a panorama of the town, such as it was, past oversize windows on the other. The woman next to me, who had earlier asked what I was reading before going on to tell me that this was her ninth jury call, for seven of which she'd been chosen, said "They have this and *Sleepless in Seattle*. They go back and forth."

The first hour was coffee and little cakey things that had been assembled back about the time the movie was opening at a theater near you. In the second hour, like good contestants we moved up a tier, escorted single file and *Quietly please* to room 3-B where we huddled in the hallway awaiting whatever negotiations transpired within. Finally admitted to perch on hard benches around a kind of arena, we heard bare details of the case: Following a domestic dispute that had neighbors calling 911, a woman had slammed out of the house, jumped into her car and rapidly backed down the drive, taking no notice of and crushing the skull of her four-year-old playing there. The police arrived to find her crouched over the body.

When my turn came for the arena seat (we were now into the third hour) I went down the checklist from the board at the front of the room. Name, age, residence, how long there, married or single, profession. The defense attorney's head came up at the last, and he asked if on a regular basis I cared for victims of domestic abuse, for the severely injured, and for the families of same. Shortly thereafter I was excused, *National Treasure* starting back up as I passed through the waiting room to surrender my juror badge.

I went straightaway to the hospital. Each afternoon from two till four, swimming upstream of phone calls, lab and X-ray techs, visitors and volunteers, the nurses do their best to enforce quiet hour. Arrived at the near end of that, I trod as seemly as possible through hallways evidently designed to pick up the tiniest sound and send it racketing from wall to wall. The two patients I'd planned on seeing were asleep, so I put in time updating charts to keep Margaret in Medical Records happy, checked in at the office (where Maryanne was alone with the fish), and went home.

There, I found, Dickens was having a busy day.

He was carrying the body of a gecko around the house as though uncertain, having come this far, what was to come next. He'd put the tiny body down, nose it an inch or two across the floor, paw desultorily at it, then pick it up again and take it to another room where he'd repeat the sequence.

Time to go on pause and think deep thoughts about life and death? Dickens was trying to figure it out, maybe I should be doing the same. In the twenty-minute slam, this is where *the look* would come over my face. Ponderment. Connection. Illumination. You'd see it in my eyes, hear it in the sound track. For moments nothing would move.

Slams aside, physicians rarely stand around thinking about death. It's just there at our shoulder, like air, water, sadness, loss, and there's always too much to do. We're problem solvers, engineers. Keep the engines running. We do *this* because, then we do *that* because. Following sequences not unlike Dickens's with the gecko.

Yet this body being carried around by Dickens, this tiny individual being, had possessed a beauty, organization and wonder far beyond that of any painting, music, grand machine or city that humankind might create. And now, abitrarily, to no purpose whatsoever, in moments that life was gone.

Insignificant? Yes—and a catastrophe.

It's because our usual concerns are so small, my father insisted, that he'd been drawn to science fiction and fantasy. Because it forces us to pull back, to look again at what we think, what we see. I first heard that when I was ten or so, in a room at a convention hotel in Cleveland, a closed party, mostly writers and high-octane fans. There was a lot of insisting going on. Someone from the group everyone called the kids, could have been Bob Silverberg, was saying here's what we've come to: science fiction's great promise of technology that was going to lead inexorably to a shining future has instead led us to the edge of destruction.

Mr. Heinlein was there. (I could never think of him otherwise.) I'd just read *Have Space Suit—Will Travel* and wanted to talk to him about it. *He* wanted to talk about *The Moon Is a Harsh Mistress*. Years later I read that one too, recognizing in its sham constitutional convention, supposed anarchic government and secret ruling elite a distorted reflection of the world I was beginning to perceive around me.

So there was in Mr. Heinlein's novel that screed of a world beneath the surface, beneath appearance. And in the same breath an unquestioned belief that our resourceful, headstrong protagonist would prevail. He'd solve all problems and get society up and running again on its true course.

Good engineer!

I don't recall what other stops my thoughts took as they scuffled along and, memory obsessively self-editing as it does, probably the chain above is tampered with as well, resequenced, but by the time Richard got home I was thinking about Phil Klein, dead thirty years. Feet firmly planted in the low-end original-paperback market, Belmont and the like, he was a popular writer, a shy man with a sweet, light touch to his tales of vain robots, OCD aliens resembling large hedgehogs who came to Earth to trade their worthless gold for something useful, and the singing cockroaches of Sigma-7. Then everything fell apart at once. His wife left him for an insurance salesman, his agent shut down shop, the editor on whom he most depended without explanation stopped answering his calls, he tumbled down stairs at his fifth-floor walk-up and was housebound with two broken legs, wholly dependent on neighbors and friends, helplessly in debt for medical care. When the legs healed, he hobbled to StopOver Hardware and bought two large tarps, laid them out on the floor, sat down in one of his two black suits, and shot himself in the head.

I'd never mentioned Phil Klein to Richard, had no cause to. Nor had I thought of the man in years. But now, sketching in what I could reconstruct of the crooked path I took to get there, I told Richard the story.

Dickens meanwhile had lost interest in his prey. Richard looked at it where it lay on the threshold, half in the living room, half in the kitchen.

"All that from a dead gecko? But I'm relieved. You didn't kill anyone today. I was fearful you had, to be in this morbid mood. Might a glass of wine help?"

"I suspect it would."

"And my patented bright repartee to go with. Carry your mournful thoughts outside and I'll be right there with the goods."

"The goods? I thought we were only having wine."

"Ah . . . feeling better already."

"Hope you don't mind my dropping by like this," Sheriff Hobbes said. Dark was sliding unobtrusively in, like a letter under the door. I'd been gearing up to get back to the hospital to see the patients I'd missed that afternoon when they were sleeping. We heard the gate and looked up.

"Knocked and didn't get an answer around front and both cars were here, so I came on back."

"There's a doorbell," Richard said.

"Never much cared for them."

"I know, what *will* they think of next? And such a waste of electricity."

The sheriff gave him a look I imagine he dispenses liberally to the town's teenagers each weekend. "Heard about that test of yours."

"One essay question," Richard offered in response to my unspoken question. "And one word: *entitlement*."

"Also understand"—the sheriff again—"you got some hassle for it."

"That I did. Along with some killer essays."

"Emerson smiles," I said. "What can we do for you, Roy?"

The sheriff put his hand on the trunk of the nearest elm and pushed gently against it, did the same about a foot higher. "Healthy tree. Firm."

"Richard's work. Trees or people, we're all happy hereabouts."

"S'pose we are, most days." The sheriff brushed off the other chair and sat. We looked like apartment dwellers lounging pool-side, or like three old guys planted in their chairs outside the care home.

"I spoke with the Rayburn boy, Lamar. Met up with a man out in the woods, he says. Richard brought the boy home, but he wasn't the one out there, was he?"

"Nathan didn't say?"

"Told me he promised not to."

"Then his promise should hold for me as well."

"Lot of promises floating around."

Dickens scratched at the patio door. Richard went to open it for him.

"Think that man would still be out there if someone were to go looking for him?"

"That's two questions. Would he be there? I don't know. Would you find him if you went looking? No."

Dickens had waddled out, plopped down by the sheriff's feet, and found the smell of his boot fascinating.

"Agreed I'd be sure to pass it along if Bobby showed up again, or if I heard anything more of him. That was a promise too.

But"—He bent down and scratched Dickens's head—"I don't expect Agent Ogden is sitting by her phone over in Richmond waiting for my call."

The sheriff's age showed as he stood to go. Legs slow to take his weight. A moment of disequilibrium once he'd hauled himself up.

Roy had his heart attack that night around 2 AM.

23

IT WAS HIS second, the first one three years back a practice run, this one down and dirty. He hadn't been taking his daily aspirin, hadn't been exercising, hadn't been eating right—living on sandwiches and frozen dinners. I soon learned why.

We had him stable and upstairs in ICU by the time dawn began easing up the windows. Richard called to see how it was going and brought in bagels, which we ate in the cafeteria, on his way to school. Afterward I visited my neglected patients. Roy was awake by then but only mildly responsive. I sat and chatted with him anyway, none of which he later remembered, went to the office to see patients there, nothing remarkable, mostly routine visits, then came back to the hospital late afternoon.

Pale and jittery as is so often the case, Roy kept picking at his gown and shifting inches right, inches left, on the pillow. But his eyes were clear.

"Guess Sam's in the driver's seat now," he said. "More than he bargained for."

His deputy had been on duty when, shortly before losing consciousness and unable to speak, Roy dialed the station. Sam radioed for the ambulance and met them there. He and Andrew had started CPR.

"Did what I could to get him ready. Day had to come."

"He'll do fine."

"Let's hope the worst of the excitement's over." Over with him—or with the town? A mass grave, unidentifiable bodies, youngsters' re-creations, shootings, strings of outsiders. Roy glanced at the monitor by his left shoulder. "Lot of numbers and squiggles."

"Good ones."

"Owe you, Lamar."

"I'll have the lecture about taking care of yourself ready once you're feeling better."

"No you won't, and you damn well know it."

"Okay. But it's in the script, right?" I stepped closer, put my hand on his arm. "I asked about Sue, Roy. No sign of her, Andrew says. Or of the dog. Dishes in the sink, on the coffee table in the front room. Tracked-in dirt and leaves."

Roy was silent. I waited.

"She's still in Minnesota? With her parents?"

"Iowa. Moved there, near her sister and family. It can get to be such a damn mess between people, you know, Lamar?"

I nodded. Oh yeah.

"What comes up around you," he went on, "it doesn't look much like what you're always hearing, how you can 'work things out.' You can't, and wanting to just leaves you sitting at the table with an empty bowl."

I had no homilies for him, no platitudes, only an empathy and understanding best expressed wordlessly.

Roy knew that. He felt it.

. . .

In *The Brothers Karamazov* prosecutor Kirillovich calls up the same word for the place of lowliness and degradation and that of lofty ideals. *Abyss.* He's employing religious imagery of course, and leaning hard on Aristotelian either-ors, but religious imagery is finally a form of figurative language, and Kirillovich is right that Dmitri's trapped between them—as are we all. The abyss above, the abyss below. With only crawlspaces to find relief. To be about our lives.

Though our news embargo was over and what came streaming in, damnable—"all those yummy snacks of The World As It Is," Richard remarked—that was not what brought me to such thoughts, nor had Dickens's gecko.

One of the triggers I'd discover only later, the other I was aware of at the time.

Almost three weeks before, Gordie and I had been on the team that resuscitated a man brought in by Andrew and his new guy from the truck stop out on 104, not a local, but a trucker passing through. An elderly couple who rarely ate out, celebrating an anniversary with a shared chicken-fried steak, came across him as they walked to their car. The truck's motor was running, the driver's door open, a leg hanging out. Gordie and I were on the call list, waiting in ER when Andrew pulled in.

You could have stood there, jotted down how the code went, and published it as the manual. Mr. Arnold was intubated in record time, shocked twice, introduced to the essential chemicals, drawn and tested, adjusted, drawn and tested again. We kept him in ER four hours, then moved him up to ICU.

And there he remained, never having regained consciousness, ventilator drawing in other support machines, monitors, pumps, like pilot fish. Mr. Arnold had no family. The shipping company sent another driver to complete his run. That was the extent of the world's notice.

So at about two in the morning, unable to sleep, again I found myself at the hospital, sitting at Mr. Arnold's bedside thinking how differently it had worked out for Roy and for him and remembering what Gordie said, that much of the time we don't help them live longer, or better, we only change the way they die. The hospital was so quiet and empty-feeling that tumbleweed blowing through the hallways wouldn't have surprised. That felt pretty much like what was going on in my mind as well.

There wasn't anything I could do, of course, and no, nothing she could get me when Sharon came in from the nurses' station to ask, and within the hour, because affixing one's unfulfillable longings to something concrete and attainable makes practical if ineffective sense, I pulled into the same parking lot Mr. Arnold had visited on his way to us, to get coffee at Bea's Diner.

She was sitting at a booth back by the kitchen doors, jean jacket over a yellow T-shirt. The diner wasn't as ghost-townish as the hospital had seemed, but the patrons sat scattered about, as though each had chosen a seat to maximize distance from every other. She smiled when she saw me, lifted a hand to point to the seat opposite her. A waiter came out from behind the counter and followed me back, menu and wipe rag in hand. I asked for coffee. Did she want anything? No.

I watched the waiter walk away. Left-leg prosthesis from about midthigh, stance belied only by the limp. Tattoo. Early thirties. Ex-military.

"Everyone said you were gone."

"I was."

"And yet."

"Exactly. And yet."

"There would seem to be little remaining here to hold the bureau's interest."

The waiter returned to tell us the coffee was stale, he was brewing a fresh pot. We thanked him.

"I'm on leave," she said. "Voluntary. Not that I'll have a job when I go back. That's how it works. Anyone who doesn't want to be there—" She finished her coffee, scummy milk floating on top; it had been sitting for some time. "You spend this huge chunk of your life getting where you want to be, busting your butt for it, then one day you look around and think—"

"That your butt doesn't so much like being busted?"

"That you're on automatic."

On his way back to the counter, the waiter (I'd caught his name tag this time: D'MITRI) stopped at a table to check on an elderly man asleep there, head almost horizontal on the back of the booth, mouth open. His Adam's apple was the size of a tennis ball.

"So here you are, at liberty. Which seems . . ."

"Random?"

"Remarkable."

"And wholly unmeditated. I got in, I drove, this is where the car stopped. All in all, not a bad place to be at liberty, given the town's history."

"Where are you staying?"

"Same as before, Best Western."

We talked on through most of the new pot of coffee. I told her about Nathan's break for freedom, Bobby showing up again, Bobby leaving again, Roy's MI, our trucker stuck in the bend between being and not. Patrons decamped, others replaced them. The sleeper woke, ordered breakfast, and promptly fell asleep again.

Upon requesting leave, Theodora told me, she cited family issues. Her superiors must know she had no family, but this was a request seldom denied. The ensuing interview took place in pure code, what was said, even body language, bearing little resemblance to what was meant.

"Four minutes in, it came to me that this was like one of those jokes you don't get, even though you know it's funny. My line supervisor did the interview. I started imagining his head blowing up like a balloon when he spoke, deflating when he stopped. It was hypnotic."

"That must have helped you get through."

"Or past."

"And now?"

"Hang out, I guess. Slow down. Talk to people. Remember."

"Sounds good. Foot's in the door, quite a world out there beyond it." I scooted to the edge of the booth. "Have to go. I left a note for Richard, and a voice mail. But he worries."

"That's good too."

She stood when I did, held back waiting for the cue, stepped forward to shake hands.

"You get tired of the Best Western and all that luxury," I said, "we have a spare room. Go native, get your Margaret Mead on."

She bent to retrieve her shoulder bag. "I did hear you and your partner are always taking in strays."

"We're strays ourselves."

"Hope *that's* not contagious." Tilting the pan, Richard pushed down on the spatula to drain before dealing portions of salmon onto our plates. Steamed zucchini and carrots waited. "First the sheriff gets sidelined. Then your friend Bobby goes off the reservation. Now Agent Ogden—out of there. You're not thinking about a sabbatical, are you? Taking up another line of work?"

"What else could I do?"

"Not a pretty picture, you sitting around the house all day musing on your ill-spent youth."

"Don't know about ill. Spent, yes. But with a few dollars left."

"And change."

"We hope."

Nathan, Richard told me, would be taking a class at the state college next semester, the extension campus at Arborville, two towns over. With a half-formed thought of finding something to engage and challenge the boy, Richard went browsing online and discovered that a woman he'd gone to graduate school with, one of the brightest people he'd ever met though surreptitiously so, "never spoke up in class, then on tests turned in these essays that read as though they'd been carved in stone," was chair of the history department. An audit was all they could swing, no credit but no charge either, and everyone was excited. The course? U.S. History: The First Year.

"You were happy to see Agent Ogden again," Richard said as we cleared the table. "Should I worry?"

"Not a heterosexual bone in my body."

"You want to know one of the first things I remember about you?"

"My charming, dangerous smile."

"One of the other things."

"Okay."

"You'd talk about people. Patients, friends, people from your past. And you'd never mention their gender. Then, we'd been together less than a month, we went to New Orleans, stayed in that hotel tucked away back behind the flower shop—Anne Street? Both owners were named Carl, and every time we went through the lobby slash office they were sniping at one another."

"They even looked alike."

"And sounded alike. Same voice, same accent, cadence."

"Visions of our own future?"

"Not even remotely. You'd told me about the washboard player at the weekend jam outside Jackson Square. What was mounted on the washboard, the cross-rhythms. Somehow you neglected to mention that she was a she, wore a tank top, and every once in a while when she got to going especially hard, her tit fell out."

"The world is filled with beautiful things."

"She'd tuck it back in, never miss a beat."

"True talent."

We'd loaded the washer and were doing a general wipe-down. Richard asked what I thought of the salmon.

"Had a bit of an edge to it."

"You're always saying it's bland and mushy, so I tried marinating it in lemon juice, pepper and white wine."

"I approve."

"We should start hitting the farmers' market again on Saturdays for veggies. Not a lot of choice in the stores right now."

"Have I told you that for years I was certain my grandfather hadn't ever eaten a vegetable? Never saw one on his plate, or on the table. Biscuits, fried meat, cornbread, potatoes, grits. Gravy."

"That was your father's dad, right?"

"Yes."

"You ever rethink the whole child thing, Lamar? How we're missing something that's such a major part of life?"

"As I've said, I never understood the pull. Never felt it. That need just got left out when I was put together. Are we missing something? I'm sure we are. But that's why we read, isn't it. Why we become involved with others. To get a sense of those lives we can't have."

Mr. Arnold, our trucker, died that night. They called from the hospital and left a message. Neither Richard nor I heard the phone.

24

MY GRANDFATHER, MY father's father, was a carpenter. He used to tell me how he'd find old pennies left under windowsills by the original builders. They were left there to date the construction—handshakes sent across the years.

We find, or conjure, what continuity we can.

Or: Three people are playing dominoes. It's a modern deck, each denomination of pips a different color. Everyone's chattering away as you play, and you begin to suspect that, while you lay down your tiles according to pip count, the player to your left is doing so in regard to color, and the player on your right sails by on pattern recognition.

Three people, all with different takes on the world, essentially *seeing* a different world.

Think of the energies required to bend those into conformance and hold them there.

Over the next weeks we had a run of flu, not a particularly virulent strain, but any flu needs watching, especially with the young, the elderly, and those compromised by chronic disease or disorder. I went to the sheriff's home to check on him. Maryanne called all our patients fitting those categories and had them come in for a quick checkup. For three days the office was full. The lab over by the college to which we sent blood work must have thought a minor epidemic had hit.

Nobody talked about the bodies anymore, or the shooting, but these were tucked away at the back of our minds and hung, if not palpably then patently, in the air we breathed. Willnot was a lake into which rocks had been thrown; mud still swirled.

Weeks went by. Late one afternoon the office had cleared out and Sheriff Hobbes showed up bearing, as he said, gifts: coffee for the two of us, and some strain of flowery-smelling tea for Maryanne.

Settled in my office, we sipped coffee as though time were on indeterminate hold and our plastic cups would never empty. Sunlight had begun to move across the floor toward the window on its way to withdrawing.

"Can't remember you ever coming here before," I said.

"Had no need."

"And now?"

He shook his head. Drank coffee.

"You know how a thing will get caught in your mind, Lamar? Not something that matters usually. Lines from a song, a place you used to live, that time you ruined your favorite shirt changing a tire. Gets where you want to tilt your head to one side like in a cartoon, beat on the other to knock it out, but it won't go."

I didn't speak, let him pace himself.

"I've been thinking about Bobby, that whole mess. Nothing about it adds up. This morning around two, three, I'm slogging through the house thinking how good a bourbon would taste. Now, that happens, a man had best find work to do. So I took a look at what had got stuck in my head and been rolling around in there. Spent the rest of the morning on the phone. The Marine Corps does not, they claim, have a soldier on any of their rosters by the name of Bobby Lowndes. Or Brandon Lowndes. FBI headquarters could confirm an agent by the name of Theodora Ogden but knew nothing about an AWOL marine."

"If he's what he says—"

"I couldn't even get someone to talk to me at the CIA number. NSA said not their bailiwick or words to that effect. Finally I called up an old friend. We served together; he went career and is still on the desk in Washington. He said let him make some calls, he'd get back to me. He did, and pretty soon too—with a big *Sorry, Roy.*"

"And you were surprised?"

"Maybe I got it out of my head. Maybe that's all the good I figured it would do. That, and just being busy. Doing something."

"You want me to make more coffee?"

"No, but thanks."

I finished mine, and put the cup beside his on the desk.

"Years ago I was catching up on reading all my father's books. One of them, *Pit Stop World*, hit a chord in me that wouldn't stop twanging. So I cited the Freedom of Information Act and requested the FBI file on my father. He'd always claimed he was just writing entertainment, but those early novels seemed to me unmistakably political. They must have seemed so to others as well. The file came in an envelope big enough to hold a family Bible, a stack of paper three or four inches high. When I began shuffling through, I found that anything of substance had been redacted in heavy black marker. All that remained were typed agent reports of contacts, "Subject said to have resided at," "Informant approached," and such. Then blocks of black. That and book reviews, many torn from fanzines cranked out on old mimeograph machines. That's about as forthcoming as I ever expect our government to be. But why is Bobby still on your mind?"

"Good question. Three nights ago I was driving around, just to get out of the house—"

"Two in the morning you're supposed to be resting after an MI, and instead you're up poking around in your head and on the phone. Now driving. What would your doctor say if he knew?"

"Well, I guess now he does. Anyway, I swung out by the highway, just rambling really, then hit some of the old back roads into town. Haven't been out there, on those, since the highway and new state road went in. Probably no one has. I'd swear the ruts I left last time are still there. I was coming slow around a long curve, had the lights off since the moon was full and it was such a beautiful night, stars every which way. That's when I saw Bobby."

"Bobby left weeks ago."

"Apparently not. Who else is going to be out there that time of night, Lamar? Or at all? And disappear like that. I hit the lights, but he was gone."

"And you're sure it was him?"

"Size, gait, the way he moved. Had to be. I went out again that afternoon and hoofed it around the area, didn't come across anything. Camp, caches, evidence of buried refuse."

"I'd be surprised if you did."

"But he's out there, Lamar. Why is he still here?"

Hope my having been here doesn't bring anything else on you, Bobby had said. I saw him standing on the porch, light from the kitchen reaching out weakly into the yard and letting go, a single cricket somewhere down in the floorboards sounding big as a badger. *I'd better get along.*

156

25

RECENT EVENTS HAVE caused me to think about my months in rehab, what it was like not to be able to hold on to a cup, stand, or put shoes on, the concentration required to perform even the most routine tasks of daily life. That night I was reliving it in dreams—something that back then never happened—when the doorbell rang.

"Oh goody! Maybe it's the matching Nixon and Bush masks I ordered for us," Richard said.

I looked at the clock. We'd been in bed less than an hour. Images of frailty and infirmity bled back from my dreams.

"I don't think UPS or FedEx deliver at eleven PM."

"Then it's a stranger come to beg a meal—"

"Thank you, Mr. Guthrie."

It was indeed a stranger, a plain woman, fifty, sixty, wearing dark slacks with some stretch to them, a light-blue shirt beneath an unbuttoned cardigan that hit at her waistline. The air had gone a bit cold; her breath made faint ghosts in the porch light.

"Doctor Hale?"

I nodded.

"Please forgive me for disturbing you, and especially at this time of night. I'm Jo Bielecki, we live up the street. On the corner, with the add-on second story on stilts?"

The old Haversham place.

"It's my father's, actually, but I'm there seeing after him. And he's why I'm here at your door. Dad's been ill for some time. Came back here, he says, like a cat climbing up under the porch—though I told him nonsense and not to keep saying that. But tonight . . ."

Attracted by the porch light, insects swirled about. She waved them away from her face, pushing left to right with one hand as though against a curtain.

"I went in to check on him. An hour ago when I looked in, he was asleep, or as close to sleep as he gets. But then when I came back, his breathing was shallow and irregular—labored. And he won't respond."

"Did you call for an ambulance?"

She shook her head. "He has a living will—though he laughed every time anyone used that term. And he was very specific. No heroic measures, no life support, no hospital. But could you come have a look at him? I can't help but wonder if there's something we might do. Something to help him, ease his suffering."

I grabbed a heavy flannel shirt from the coat stand by the door, asked her to wait a moment while I told Richard where I was going. She and I walked silently along dead-quiet streets, the moon nodding in and out of clouds. When I was a child and we first moved to Willnot, the Haversham place was another plain-vanilla home like most from the town's founding, a bungalow really, then bit by bit over the years it grew, new rooms spliced onto the rear, a carport and outbuilding added, that weird second story. Residency seemed forever in flux. People moved into it like hermit crabs, stayed awhile, moved out to make room for others.

158

"Dad lived here when he was young," my companion said as I followed her up four stairs. Three stout men could stand side by side on the porch. The fourth would be out of luck. "Stuart Bielecki. He built it."

"And a lot of the town as well."

"Youthful folly, he always said."

"Youthful folly doesn't often create things that are still standing three generations later."

She opened the front door, and as I stepped in, the smell of dampness, mold and rotting wood came to me.

Pale green light somewhere across the room. Damp-animal smell of a humidifier whose filter badly needed changing. A hand on my arm—my daughter's, Jo's—and when I looked down it was like a catcher's mitt holding a stick. Not much left of me.

Something I had to do.

I knew then why I was dreaming of infirmities, why so many images of death had been floating about me, why the thought of Kirillovich's abyss had drifted back after so many years.

I had been here before.

"Dad's in the bedroom, at the back," she said.

But I knew that.

At the door she thought to hold back, then, revising that thought, stepped in ahead of me. She put her hand gently on his arm. "Dad, this is Dr. Hale. Your neighbor. Is it okay if he looks at you?"

I crossed to the bed, strangely in two places at once, there on the bed, in memory at least, and here walking toward it.

But it was more than memory. And even as in anticipation my mind ticked down the familiar checklist, breathing, heart rate, skin temp, pupils, pain response, I knew that was unnecessary.

A tall man, a stranger, stands beside me. Dr. Hale, she says. I look up at him and try to speak. Can't. The man nods. I know, he tells me.

I wanted to see what had become of the town. If all of it meant anything. I guess our lives mean what we want them to, what we make of them. That's what Daniel used to say, anyway. He was the smart one, always talking about market forces and capital, how they'd trump whatever government happened to be around. Grind it right down, he'd say. Woops, there goes democracy. There goes a kind society that takes care of its aged, its infirm. Heady stuff. And head in the clouds.

Sometimes you just have to *do things*, you know?

What's important—that's what you keep your eye on. What needs to be done and how to get from here to there. What you can't get around, you remove. Committees will fill a bucket with spit but they won't pick the damn thing up and carry it, the weight of it. And someone has to.

If only I could believe in anything now, anything at all, the way I did back then.

The bodies can't be theirs, I know that. They'd be long gone. But when Jo read the news story to me, it was like the town was calling me. My past was calling me back. And I knew that coming here was the last thing I had to do.

The tall man beside the bed bends down, his hand on my arm. Like Jo's. So much is spilling out from within me.

I'll wait with you, he says.

26

FOLLOWING WEEKS WERE the précis over which you labor, mind backpedaling to cram in whatever might be important, or the résumé that squats on the screen, cursor blinking, as you fuss over whether to include that honors program during college days. A dozen people stacked like planks into a phone booth, thirteen clowns emerging from a VW, the commercial that keeps you away from the show. As time gobbled up the hours.

Roy went back to work half days and, as far as I could tell, stuck to our agreement that he limit himself to such. Riding the desk and phone, as he put it.

Agent Ogden called close to midnight on a Thursday to tell me that she was returning to Richmond, leaving in minutes, in fact. Dark outside, murky future, she'd turn on the lights, drive, and see. I wished her luck.

Nathan, mom and sister had dinner with us, for which Richard "assembled" a shepherd's pie and broiled asparagus, and at which no one mentioned the boy's aborted desertion as Nathan filled every chink in conversation with talk about his upcoming class at the college. He had been reading the course catalog daily, his mother said. Reminded her how as a child in a trailer park in Texas she spent hours poring over the Sears catalog. *That* was the real world, she'd thought then. So much fine, classy stuff, the stuff of dreams, of the good life. Though of course it wasn't, really most of it was on the cheap, plywood and glue and glitter. Then, realizing at some level how oddly her reminiscence rang against her son's enthusiasm, she grew silent. At which point sister Chloe told us she wanted to go to college too. When I asked Nathan if he'd seen Bobby, he paused before saying "Once."

Jo Bielecki closed down the Haversham place and left town, back to Tacoma where she'd lived twenty years ago, she said, after burying her father in Willnot as he'd asked. It got out who the old man was, and half the town showed up for the service. Andrew, wearing a new, well-fit dark suit and starched white shirt complete with cuff links, headed things up. A FOR SALE sign appeared briefly on the front lawn of the house, then quietly vanished. The house remained empty.

I never discussed what happened that night, sketching out only the shape of the night's events for Richard, who chose not to give voice to the questions alight in his eyes. For all the lives I'd dipped into, never had I felt so intimate a bond. I understood that I'd been given something immeasurably private, something of a value beyond imagination.

Barely had we finished talking and, with dawn blushing in the windows, begun to get ready for a few hours' sleep, when Richard called from the bedroom.

Dickens was on the bed seizing, all four legs tonic, jaws snapping. Bladder and bowels had emptied. Froth and traces of vomit hung from his mouth. We sat on opposite sides of the bed touching him, waiting for the convulsions to subside.

162

Over past months I'd taken note of Dickens's increasing thirst and urination, figured in his lethargy and vomiting, and come up with feline diabetes, which Dr. Levy would soon confirm, and which with a high-fiber, high-carb diet and insulin would go into remission. Of late I'd begun to suspect tumors as well.

I'd been reluctant to say anything to Richard but now told him my conclusion and speculation, running down the options.

"Is there anything else we can do?" he asked.

"What we do already. Be with him. Care."

The contractions had stopped, and Dickens looked blankly around—lost, or reorienting. He twisted till he got his back legs under him and tried to stand, but promptly collapsed and lay there panting. Three more tries and he made it. Wobbling, with legs still shaky, he walked to Richard and climbed into his lap.

Time's appetite held, and days were consumed.

Dickens rallied and soon was himself again, logging serious rest time to re-collect energy for trips to food bowl and litter box. His new favorite place (the loci of these changed frequently—Richard called them his roosts) was the bedroom clothes hamper, and he seemed to be there whenever access was required, so that soiled clothes accumulated on the floor alongside. Through these, to attain his perch, Dickens trod disdainfully.

For a brief period, stories flourished of dead rats, dozens of them it was said, come upon at the dump, behind the elementary school, by the town reservoir. With investigation the stories proved to derive from discovery of a single rat and a couple of field mice, bell-curving as they passed from person to person, gone by week's end. Interestingly, during the stories' currency we experienced, both at office and at hospital, gaggles of patients with pedestrian complaints, coughs and rashes and the like, they'd heard might be symptoms of worse disease.

Richard arrived home from administrative meetings late one afternoon railing at budget cuts that threatened extracurriculars, band and chorus among them. "No pay raises for my teachers, either," he says, "but you'll be glad to hear the football and basketball teams are safe."

Another day I came home to find Nathan sitting outside under the Chinese elm, attention sunk fathoms deep in a copy of Theodor Adorno's *Minima Moralia: Reflections from Damaged Life*. He had discovered the Frankfurt School and really, really needed to talk to Richard about it.

Not long after that, we both got hit by a blue-ribbon cold that moved in for better than a week and would not let go, groans and coughs resounding from kitchen to living room, bedroom to bath. Dove calls, Richard termed them. I took to wearing a dapper lime-green surgical mask around the office, which afforded me a middling cachet but did little else besides make the patients feel better, and I kept away from the hospital. Richard of course claimed that's where I brought it home from in the first place. I in turn put the blame on his kids. It was an old and unfunny joke that nonetheless stayed around, like tack hanging in long-abandoned stables.

The day came when I woke without my first thought being what will hurt most today and took a deep breath without having to bound from bed to deal with throat-ripping coughs. Residual soreness from cramps, but nothing new as I cautiously stretched. Gut still sending cease-and-desist messages from all the acetaminophen, herb tea, expectorants, juice and guaifenesin I'd doused it with. But the virus was dearly departed.

Richard stood in the kitchen peering into an omelet pan as though it were a handheld mirror. He had on his favorite

Bullwinkle pajamas, which he never wore when ill, in which case it was strictly Goodwill T-shirt and sweats. Celebratory, then.

"So, you too?" I said.

"Shhh. Not aloud!" He glanced around, at nothing, conspiratorily. "How's your gut?"

"I'm thinking a sea serpent may have taken up residence."

"Then a chili omelet's just the thing. Fix you right up."

Richard's chili omelet was not the only surprise that week.

Mother had come across a huge cache of my father's books, sixty-four of them, in a used book store so overwrought, she said, that she walked between shelves fearful that any moment they might topple and crush her, and sent the lot of them to me. These represent, I think, the bulk of his novels, tilting somewhat toward fantasy. Though the bookstore owner told Mother they'd all come from a single collector, many were signed to Walters and Bridgets and Emilys and Biggest Fans. Fully half bore a bookplate with a wizard in sparkly gown and peaked hat sitting with legs crossed on a recliner reading. The name on the bookplate, Mother said in a note, she remembered, associating it with a vague, expressionless young woman who followed them around at conventions but never spoke.

Among the books, I read for the first time *The Biographer*, his story of a man who purloins people from their lives, tucks them away (where, we never learn, nor does it matter) while he takes their places and, after twenty to thirty pages, releases them back into lives dramatically changed by his actions (things they would never do) and his experiences (experiences they would never have, that remained with them upon reoccupation) during his tenure.

The man's name is Benito, who speaks both in voice-over and, during residencies, in the voice of the person he's become. He writes that he is a man without properties, a man who can be anyone but is ultimately no one. "I have been doing this a thousand years, have led hundreds upon hundreds of lives. Every one was as large from inside, and as small from outside, as every other. Each man's or woman's life is a world. I touch down, and fly away again into the void."

Richard has come up and watched over my shoulder as I wrote the last few lines. "That's one I'd like to read," he says. "Dinner will be ready in fifteen." I listen to him walk away, and in my mind hear his gait not as it is now that he's made so much progress, but as it was before—still, though, that heavy fall, the brushlike sound of the other foot dragged forward, not quite parting from ground, then the lighter footfall. *Cretic* in Latin poetics, one short, two long. I blink back tears.

27

DAYS LATER, A storm moved in and claimed us, the sort that brings old pans out from cabinets to catch the water breaching roofs and sends people out to their garages to check on boats, just in case. Windows went worthless, fingers drummed away at the boxes we live in, and newscasts from the capital fed repetitive footage of cars and pickup trucks with a foot or so of windshield showing above water, like the heads and eyes of alligators. Meanwhile, offstage, armies of mosquitoes waited, dreaming of glory days to come.

Schools shut down, and while the sheriff's department and hospital staff were on alert, mostly people stayed home and Willnot stayed quiet. A suspected break-in at May's Collectables proved to be the result of a door left unlocked and blown open by wind, triggering the alarm. Per custom the high school gym remained open to provide shelter.

Midafternoon, as standing water began to drain and the sun pushed its way through spongy clouds (Willnot ever avoiding the usual—having such occur, for instance, *during* the storm), we had a blackout. Could be down for hours, the power company announced. The hospital was on generators and had the situation in hand, vents up and running, auxiliary lights, batteries stockpiled for IVs and pumps, Ambu bags shucked from sealed bags and handily at bedside with respiratory, nurses and aides all prepared to bag dependent patients.

I'd sent Maryanne home and was standing at the window watching water recede, scarcely a thought in my head, adrift. I'd made coffee before the power cut out and was doing my best to drink it before it went dead cold. Light in the office reminded me of grainy old B movies, those where people's faces are a blur and that object in the background might as easily be a refrigerator, window frame or shape-shifting monster. I heard the outer door open. Moments later she stepped to the other side of my doorway and stopped, as though it were an imperceptible barrier. I half expected her to put up a hand to confirm.

"Dr. Hale?"

She wore newish jeans, a fitted blouse under a gray windbreaker, a baseball cap with hair in a ponytail pulled through the back. Midthirties? She was soaked, and her shoes squished mightily as she stepped in. Surely I imagined that, first, she took a deep breath.

"And you?"

"Ginny Farrell. I hear you're good with animals."

"Oh?"

"From kids at the park. I spend a lot of time there. I hear them talking. Can you help me?"

"With what, Ms. Farrell?"

She was quiet. Had that look of running it through one's head like a script. How to get so many connections and crossovers in the right order, down to what might make sense.

"Here." Against her body she cradled a small bundle wrapped

in a towel, which she held out and quickly brought back. "I had three miscarriages, when I was married. I was told I wouldn't be able to bear children. But now—"

It was a *very* small bundle.

Briefly the lights flickered on and off. We waited. That seemed to be it.

"—now I've given birth. This morning. As the storm was coming in." She walked to the desk, put the bundle on it, and started folding back the towel. "Isn't she beautiful?"

I looked down, then back up at her. At her eyes.

What she had, so meticulously enswathed, was a lizard the size of a chipmunk, alive but immobile with fear.

"But I can't keep her. I'm not married. And she needs a good home. I thought you could help find one for her."

I asked her to sit. She did so, rewrapping the towel and holding the bundle carefully in her lap. I said that I'd do what I could, but first we needed to get both her and the baby to the hospital to have them checked out. Went on a bit, though gently, about birth trauma, loss of blood, potential infection. She seemed to be considering it but, once I stopped talking, shook her head, saying that she had changed her mind and was going to keep the baby.

Tucking the towel more securely in place, she stood and walked to the doorway before turning back.

"They'll say I'm crazy, Dr. Hale."

Immediately I called the sheriff's department. Roy answered and, when he heard why I was calling, passed me on to Sam. Ginny Farrell lived out on the old feeder highway, Sam said. He'd been by there twice, domestic disputes. He'd head right out.

He called back within the hour. No one home, no one around. Spoke to the neighbors, who couldn't remember seeing Ginny for some time, then returned to the house and found the back door unlocked. Looked like the lock hadn't worked for years. Inside, everything was tip-top. Clean and orderly and no clutter anywhere, not a chair or dish or piece of clothing out of kilter. Spooky, Sam said. Like being on a movie set or in a model home, a place conjured up whole in someone's mind but never lived in.

He went back repeatedly over the following days. The house remained as it was. Ginny Farrell didn't return. We never heard from or of her again.

Why do I tell you this, and why here? Because I've relived that visit so many times; I've not been able to put it to rest. And because of what I'm about to tell you. Because it brought to mind then, and brings to mind ever more forcefully in light of subsequent events, how little we sometimes can do to help.

28

I'D BEEN KEPT late at the hospital that day with a routine bladder tuck that step by step became anything but. Unwarranted bleeding, careening BP, a node of cancer tucked away so stealthily behind bone that it never showed on X-rays.

I parked, caught my breath and, walking in, heard voices from the kitchen. Richard and Bobby Lowndes looked up from the table.

"We saved you some tea," Richard said. He got up, took the pot and a cup already set out on the counter, and poured. A thimbleful splashed into the cup. "Woops, I guess we didn't. I can make more."

"This may be a Scotch evening."

"She okay?"

I'd had the circulating nurse call to let Richard know about the protracted surgery.

"Will be, yes. Bobby. Heard rumors you were still around."

"So he is. Finger on the pulse of." Richard went out to the front room to get the Scotch.

"Didn't mean to be," Bobby said. "Kept having reasons not to go. Finding them, I guess is the truth of the thing. But today I came to say good-byes. Already said them to Nathan."

"I won't ask where you're going."

"I know."

Richard came in with the bottle and a glass for me, set it on the table and, going back around, behind Bobby, lost his footing. He reached out to grab at Bobby's chair and I thought had caught himself, but then crashed down. It took a moment for me to register that I'd heard, just before he fell, a high-pitched whistle and crack.

Bobby was up and out the door almost before Richard hit the floor. Around the hole in the window glass I watched him disappear into the trees, understanding then what had happened.

Richard's eyes were wide, already shock-y looking, and there was, for so small an entry wound, far too much blood.

Much of it's a blur. I remember pushing against his chest and diaphragm, breathing into his slack mouth. Yellow dish towels going red with blood. Like peasants with pitchforks up against armies, I fought with what I had. I remember pulling down the cutlery drawer for a good knife, then pulling out the drawer where we stored cheesecloth and trussing twine and dumping its contents on the floor. My fingers on bleeders. Lurching for the phone and punching numbers with one hand as the other went on doing what I've done all these years.

So much of it was automatic.

So much of it was, or seemed at the time, in vain.

At some point Bobby is there saying It's taken care of, I should never have come here, brought all this, good luck to you both, Dr. Hale. Then a flash, a darkness, he's gone, and Andrew stands above me in his dark suit and cuff links with the ambulance outside in the driveway, the front door open, the sheriff and Sam walking through it.

I'm in the ambulance. Bagging Richard. Starting an IV.

Andrew and I pushing the stretcher through the ER door, people parting left and right, faces stark in the sudden light, pages sounding overhead.

I'm outside OR. Gordie's telling me that it was touch and go at first but all is going well now, he's stable. I notice that Gordie doesn't take his eyes off mine. I notice that he's wearing his lucky scrub cap—with the plaid of his clan.

I came awake sitting by Richard's bed in intensive care. Eyes at half-mast, he was watching me. The room dark, a wash of light from outside, from the nurses' station and unit proper, that lost force before it reached us. Steady tick of his QRS on the monitor. "They tell me you saved my life," he said. "If I say thank you, will you go home and get some rest?" Later, I wondered if I dreamed that.

Later also, Roy and Sam came to tell me they'd found the shooter just yards into the woods behind the house. His throat had been slit, one swift, expert strike. He'd died instantly. The killer took care to arrange the body on its back, straight, as though at rest, rifle tucked alongside. Perfect right shoulder arms, Roy said.

Slowly time, or memory, congeals. Richard on his back, face locked in concentration as he wills his leg to bend, to slide his foot toward him, and it begins, very slightly, to move. At the end of the hall tottering in his walker as he turns. He reaches out to the wall to steady himself and misjudges, almost goes down. Holding hard to the bars on either side as he attempts to walk again for the first time. Leg lifts and squats and stair steps that leave him all but breathless and shiny with sweat. All too well I remember what it was like.

Richard saying they tell me I'm out of the woods and the other guy never got out of them. Gordie coming out from OR to say

Richard was in Recovery and everything looked good. Hypoxia's the monkey in the gears though, he says, and we don't know the extent of it. Metabolic encephalopathy for sure. Permanent damage or loss, we don't know, we'll just have to wait. And Kate Cross at University Hospital: It's going to be a long haul, Lamar, you know that. But he's going to be okay. Conservatively? Eighty percent recovery.

So, refusing to tune ahead in our minds, we wrestle the hour, hour after hour, and days fall away. Then weeks. We work his butt ragged, we make arrangements to continue rehab with home visits and half days at University in the capital, then one day we're home.

For the first two weeks Dickens scarcely left Richard's side. He moved onto the bed, stayed beside him, and would not budge or be budged, even to eat. I took in food for him on the same tray as Richard's meals and set up a litter box at bedside. Richard, of course, asked if the litter box was for him.

29

A YEAR LATER, Richard went back to teaching. It wasn't easy for him, but then nothing in the last year and a half had been. And it's still not. The limp got better but it's there and always will be, and I still listen for it, even when he's two rooms away. There are days when his hand won't do as bid, when he drops or crushes what he tries to hold, days when words, mostly proper nouns but sometimes *shirt* or *schedule* or *sandwich*, flee him. They walk the plank of my tongue and leap off the side to oblivion, Richard says. And: Each day is a gift—in tacky wrapping paper.

So each day I'm reminded of what we can do, and the limits of it. And the hours surprise me with reminders of how close Richard and I have become, for it's as though, physically and emotionally, I was with him through every moment of pain, of fear, of disability.

Half days worked so well for Richard at University Hospital that I decided they'd suit me too, so when I went back to work, I cut my patient load and time in the office, and scheduled OR only on Mondays. One of the new arrivals had taken care of my patients while I was away. Some stayed with her, some returned, some strayed to other physicians. Maryanne was kept busy for a while forwarding medical records, after which she decided she liked the new hours too, worked when I did, and had the rest of her time free.

After one semester of audit and two of provisional classwork, Nathan was offered early admission to the university and a scholarship. His mother moved the family there, where she landed a job as hostess at one of the best restaurants in town.

During convalescence, Richard wrote a novel, *Deadline*—with, he said, no agenda or motive save to keep himself occupied and on focus. It began with a writer much like my father standing on his ragged porch reading a letter from, he had supposed, a fan.

Dear Paul Bleating,

Recently I have been commissioned by the New York Times *to write your obituary. I have of course done my homework, as it were, and fully plan on discussing your early development as a romance writer under numerous bylines, the importance of the nonfiction you contributed to* Popular Mechanics, *the origin and creation of your much-neglected novel* Whatsit— *among much else.*

I have one question for you.

Can you tell me when you plan to die? I work much better with a deadline.

Sincerely,
Simon Rapaport

P.S. Also, I need the money.

I read it one late afternoon sitting at the kitchen table where so much had happened. I had no idea this was what he had been doing with his time. Every word and page was unmistakably, indelibly Richard. It went from weird to funny to funny weird. Don Westlake would have loved it.

Scattered throughout were misread signs, and caricatures of people we knew: the anonymous driver of Big Orange the VW, Sheriff Roy (who came off a lot like Jim Thompson's sheriffs from *The Killer Inside Me* and *Pop. 1280* without the cruelty and psychosis), a couple of our recent mayors, a mysterious female federal agent named Bobbie, a tap-dancing doctor who for hundreds of years had appeared from nowhere whenever need was great, saved and repaired lives, then vanished.

"Okay," Richard said when I put the last page facedown. He'd done his best to stay out of the room as I read, but materialized every half hour to ask if I needed anything, eyes furtively weighing my progress.

"It's good. Funny. You know that."

"Okay."

"I do think one writer in a person's life may be enough."

"Hey, it kept me off the streets and out of trouble. And it's not like I plan to make a habit of it—I'm done. Considering taking up the banjo next, maybe move on to ceramics after that."

"Then I hope you'll come and visit once you've moved."

"Hmmmm. Maybe I need to rethink this."

One day not long after, Richard met me at the door with "Something for you on the kitchen table. Not dinner—that'll be along in due time. Soon as I due it." With which he clomped back to the pantry to stand looking at shelves waiting for inspiration to strike.

Leaned against the laptop that wandered about the house being used by both of us, was a postcard of some ageless small town (Montana, maybe?) consisting, it seemed, solely of a main street, dwarfed by mountains behind and clouds above.

Remember the old joke about the translation of out of sight, out of mind? Invisible and insane.

Or an old sf story about people who live forever but every hundred years have to go in and have their memories erased?

What I wish sometimes.

I used to sleep a lot. But once you wake up—

It was unsigned, and didn't need to be. No one would ever again hear from Bobby.

One last thing.

We buried Dickens yesterday. In our backyard the sun shone, and a new brood of crickets, trying on their new lives for a fit, leapt up tentatively into the wind, into the world.

A NOTE ON THE AUTHOR

James Sallis is the author of more than two dozen volumes of fiction, poetry, translation, essays, and criticism, including the Lew Griffin cycle and *Drive*, *Cypress Grove*, *Cripple Creek*, *The Killer Is Dying*, and *Salt River*. His biography of the great crime writer Chester Himes is an acknowledged classic. Sallis lives in Phoenix, Arizona, with his wife, Karyn.

ML   7-16